"Why didn't yo...
Dylan demande...

"I . . . I was afraid."

"Afraid? Afraid of what? That I wouldn't believe the baby was mine?"

"No," Chantal told him honestly. "That never crossed my mind."

If nothing else, that convinced him she was telling the truth. "What, then?"

"There were a lot of reasons I didn't call sooner, but there's no sense getting into that now. I called you because you're a cop, and I thought you could help."

Like everything else she'd said, the statement made little sense, but there was a forlorn quality to her words that tugged at the heartstrings he didn't even know he had anymore. "I'm not following you. You thought I could help with what?"

"Dylan, someone stole our baby."

Dear Reader,

Happy New Year! May this year bring you happiness, good health and all that you wish for. And at Silhouette Special Edition, we're hoping to provide you with a year full of books that are chock-full of happiness!

In January, don't miss stories by some of your favorite authors: Curtiss Ann Matlock, Myrna Temte, Phyllis Halldorson and Patricia McLinn. This month also brings you *Far To Go*, by Gina Ferris—a heartwarming addition to her FAMILY FOUND series.

The January selection of our THAT SPECIAL WOMAN! promotion is *Hardhearted* by Bay Matthews. This is the tender tale of a woman strong enough to turn a gruff, lonely, hardhearted cop into a true family man. Don't miss this moving story of love. Our THAT SPECIAL WOMAN! series is a celebration of our heroines—and the wonderful men they fall in love with. THAT SPECIAL WOMAN! is friend, wife, lover—she's each one of us!

In Silhouette Special Edition, we're dedicated to publishing the types of romances that you dream about— stories that delight as well as bring a tear to the eye. That's what Silhouette Special Edition is all about— special books by special authors for special readers.

I hope that you enjoy this book and all the stories to come.

Sincerely,

Tara Gavin
Senior Editor

BAY
MATTHEWS
HARDHEARTED

Silhouette ®

SPECIAL EDITION ®

Published by Silhouette Books
America's Publisher of Contemporary Romance

SILHOUETTE BOOKS

ISBN 0-373-09859-6

HARDHEARTED

BAY MATTHEWS

of Haughton, Louisiana, describes herself as a dreamer and an incurable romantic. Married at an early age to her high school sweetheart, she claims she grew up with her three children. Now that only the youngest is at home, writing romances adds an exciting new dimension to her life.

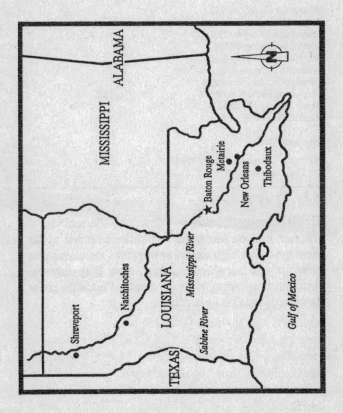

Chapter One

Chantal Robichaux gazed down in loving adoration at the red and wrinkled face of the baby lying next to her, admiring the abundance of dark hair, adoring his button nose and the fragile sweep of wispy eyelashes lying against plump cheeks, marveling at the miracle of conception, the miracle of birth. A humbling surge of love washed through her. How could she have entertained the slightest doubt about the wisdom of keeping him? He was hers. Her son. Hers to love, to care for, to shape into a mature adult—frightening responsibilities, but responsibilities she was more than willing to undertake in spite of the circumstances of his birth.

"He's beautiful, sis," Cade Robichaux said, tracing a gentle finger over the whorl of satin-soft hair that marked the crown of the baby's head.

"Wonderful." The singular comment came from Shiloh, who had been her brother's wife for almost two years.

Chantal, who was still weary from the baby's birth eleven hours before and groggy from the pain medication she was taking, felt her eyes fill with tears. "He's just...perfect, isn't he?"

"Has all of his fingers and toes, does he?" Cade teased.

"I counted them twice just to make sure," Chantal admitted with a look of chagrin. The teasing note in her voice disappeared. "After all the things you hear that can go wrong, it's such a miracle that he's okay, that he's..." her voice trailed away on a cracked note. She gazed into her son's face. "He might not have been planned, but he certainly wasn't unwanted."

"At least not after the initial shock wore off," Cade reminded her.

Remembering her dismay at finding she was pregnant without a husband brought a rush of memories Chantal didn't want to think about just now. Yet no matter how much she might want to deny Dylan Garvey's part in the baby's conception, it was a bitter reality, as undeniable as the sobering realization that she'd fallen so fast and so hard for Dylan only to learn that, like her father and the other men she'd trusted— men who'd taken her heart and lied to her—Dylan, too, had feet of clay.

Chantal threw off the troubling thoughts. She didn't want to think about any of that now. She wanted to revel in the pleasure of the baby sleeping so contentedly in her arms. Wanting, needing, to touch him, she leaned forward. There was a sudden pain in her abdomen, the result of the C section that was necessitated by his nine-pound, one-ounce size. Ignoring the discomfort, she brushed her dry lips against the incredible softness of his head. He squirmed, stretched, made a mewling noise and pursed his tiny lips . . . lips that were shaped exactly like his father's.

"Oh, look, Cade!" Shiloh exclaimed. "Isn't he adorable?"

"He looks like Dylan," Chantal said without thinking. The ticking of the utilitarian clock hanging on the opposite wall echoed loudly in the sudden silence that filled the room. She looked into her brother's set features. Cade was of the opinion that Dylan should be informed of his child's existence, a stand he had taken from the first.

"I know what you're thinking," she said.

"And?"

Chantal expelled a harsh breath. "And, as I've said a dozen times before, I think that telling Dylan about the baby would stir up more problems than I can handle right now."

"That baby is his son, too, Chantal."

"I know that."

"I'd be madder than hell if I was in his shoes."

"Cade . . ."

"Do you have a name picked out?"

Chantal glanced up at her sister-in-law with genuine relief. She knew the question was a diversionary tactic, that Shiloh hoped to ease the tension binding the trio of adults.

"I have two or three in mind," she said, "but I haven't decided yet."

"Hello."

Chantal's attention shifted from Shiloh to the door. The singsong greeting came from a plump woman attired in the familiar hospital aide's garb of pastel blue pants and coordinating floral top. She smiled, and the action wrought deep crow's feet at the corners of her small blue eyes. "How's it going?"

"Fine."

A look of regret edged aside the woman's smile. "I hate to break up the party," she said, approaching the bed on crepe-soled shoes, "but I need to take your little man away for a while."

Chantal's hold on the baby tightened instinctively. As tired as she was, she wasn't ready to give him up just yet. "Is everything all right?" she asked the woman whose name tag read: Ann Gordon, Nurse's Assistant.

"Everything's just fine. The pediatrician is here and wants to do the baby's circumcision," the aide said, her bright eyes meeting Chantal's before she bent over to pick up the baby.

"Oh." The absence of her son's warmth left Chantal with a sudden, bone-deep chill. She watched the woman nestle him in the crook of her arm with enviable ease and a bit of possessiveness that was somehow irritating. She chided herself for the uncharitable thought. Just because she felt insecure and inadequate when she handled the baby didn't give her any cause to be jealous of other people's proficiency.

"You did want him circumcised, didn't you?" Ann Gordon asked.

"Yes, of course."

"Good." She flashed Chantal a smile and turned to Cade and Shiloh. "Tell everyone bye-bye," she cooed to the child in her arms.

"Bye, Baby," Shiloh and Cade said in tandem. They laughed, then Shiloh turned to Chantal, adding, "You've really got to name him soon. We can't keep calling him Baby."

"I know, I know." She shifted her gaze from her family to the door that was swishing shut behind the woman and her son. Explaining the sudden emptiness that enveloped her would have been impossible. She supposed it had something to do with finally getting at least part of her heart's desire...a child. The other part—a man who was honest and true and who would love her as much as she loved him—remained elusive. She was beginning to wonder if there was such a critter out there in the big cruel world.

"You look tired," Shiloh said, her dark eyebrows drawn together in concern. "We should leave."

"Don't go," Chantal protested. "I'm fine."

"Shiloh's right," Cade said. "Besides, we didn't come to see you, anyway. We came to see the baby."

"Cade!"

His grin was unrepentant. "Lighten up, *chère*," he said, before dropping a brief kiss to his wife's mouth. "Chantal knows I'm just pulling her leg." He leaned over the bed and kissed his sister's pale cheek. "You get some sleep. We'll stop by tonight for a few minutes."

Chantal nodded. They were right. She was tired. But it was a good tired, almost as good as the weariness she'd felt after she and Dylan made love. She pushed the unwelcome thought aside and said her goodbyes. Soon she was left alone in her narrow bed with an afternoon and evening stretching out before her, nothing to do but rest and try to hold the memories at bay...memories of the night she'd met Dylan Garvey....

It promised to be the longest six weeks Chantal Robichaux had ever lived through, and considering that she'd only been in Atlantic City for five interminable days—and nights—it seemed to get longer all the time.

When Shiloh, her new sister-in-law of less than a year, had asked if she'd be interested in coming to Atlantic City to oversee her family's casino while the elder Ramblers spent six weeks in Europe, Chantal had declined, even though she'd been without a steady job for five months—ever since the hotel she had managed had filed bankruptcy. The offer smacked of charity, and besides, Chantal had reminded Shiloh, running a gambling casino was a far cry from managing a hotel. Shiloh had insisted, saying that her father would be happier with "family" in charge. The way she saw it, Chantal filled the bill all the way around: she was both family and qualified.

Chantal wasn't convinced. She hated the cold, hated the north, or the East, or wherever the heck Atlantic City was. The idea of being in a city bigger than Thibodaux, Louisiana, where she'd been born, raised and would undoubtedly draw her last breath, was enough to give her the willies. There was country deep in her soul and warm bayou water coursing through her Southern veins. She also recalled Shiloh saying there had been a rash of thefts in some of the smaller casinos recently—including Rambler's—and Chantal wanted no part of that headache.

Jon Rambler had called himself, adding his plea to his daughter's. He assured her that Lyle Kennedy, Rambler's manager, could handle the bulk of the responsibility, but there was no way he could be at the casino twenty-four hours a day. In the end, despite her stiff-necked pride, Chantal had acquiesced. Her current job, working for a temporary secretarial service, hardly kept food on the table much less paid the bills...which were stacking up at an alarming rate. Even though she knew he could afford it, she hadn't been able to bring herself to borrow any more money from Cade.

And so, here she was, at Rambler's.

She looked out over the sea of people clustered around the various gaming tables and tuned out the muted rumble of voices, the whir of the roulette wheel and the tinny pings of the slot machines. "Just five more weeks," she muttered under her breath.

As she did every night, she found herself wondering what the draw was. Having been abandoned by her father at the age of eight, and having scrimped and saved most of her life, Chantal couldn't see the thrill in plunking down her hard-earned money on the whimsical roll of the dice or the off chance of drawing the right card.

If only Cade were here, she thought, a half smile curving her full lips. He'd have a ball. Though her brother had suffered the pangs of poverty along with her and their sister, Monique, he'd made a fortune by creating a series of popular video games. His marriage to Shiloh Rambler had placed him squarely in a family born to gambling, and Cade had discovered he had a liking and a flair for the pastime—or vice. Of course, he was far too disciplined ever to get carried away with his betting. Like all the Robichaux's, Cade had learned life's lessons well.

Chantal banished a fleeting pang of jealousy for Cade's happy marriage and his recent fatherhood. How could she be jealous of her brother when she knew how long he had been alone and lonely? He deserved the happiness he'd found with Shiloh. The fault for her own discontent was hers. If she suddenly found a bottle with a genie inside who could grant her heart's dearest wish, that wish would be for a husband and family. She was beginning to believe that, like the genie, her wish would never materialize.

Oh, she'd given both love and marriage a whirl. First, she fell for a college jock at twenty. When she learned that her star football player was dating not only her but a couple of other girls, she'd given him a piece of her mind in exchange for his taking a piece of her heart.

Smarter, and more cautious, she'd still dated, but casually, putting her energy into her part-time jobs and her studies. Even so, she was twenty-five before she received her business degree. And then she met Jeremy Broussard, an up-and-coming real estate broker at a party given by a friend after their college graduation. Jeremy was thirty-four, a handsome smooth-talker who had literally charmed the pants off her. They were married within six weeks.

Chantal was happier than she'd ever been in her life. She had her diploma, an exciting new husband, a challenging new job, a spanking new house and a shiny new car. Jeremy claimed he was crazy about her; she adored him. She threw herself into her new life the way she had her pursuit of her degree—with total dedication. Their marriage was eighteen months old and she was six months' pregnant when she found out Jeremy was having an affair with his blond secretary, who could have been the prototype for every blonde joke ever created.

When Chantal confronted him, he didn't bother denying the affair, assuring her that it had nothing to do with his feelings for her. Wild with grief, she'd run out of the house and flung herself into her car, even though one of the worst storms of the spring was in progress. Three miles out of town, she'd missed a turn and crashed her new car into a tree.

Though she survived, neither her baby nor her marriage did. It had taken her years to deal with the grief of her double loss, years for her independent nature to reassert itself and for her to get a portion of her self-esteem back. She dated. She had fun. But she had become wary of giving her heart again.

Since she'd lost her job, her interest in dating had waned until her social life was almost nonexistent. Back in Thibodaux, she was too busy trying to make ends meet to have fun. But now she admitted that watching the men and women at Rambler's, brushing against each other, flirting, teasing with a coy look or the lift of demure eyelashes, was unsettling. She witnessed such sights nightly at the casino, sights she'd rather not have to deal with. There was something about the looks, the touches and the smiles that fed the despair growing inside her. After all, she was pushing thirty-six—not old, but not getting any younger, either.

A woman's ecstatic squeal drew Chantal's attention to the roulette table. A flashy redhead was bouncing up and down, her generous bosom threatening to burst free of her glittering, low-cut gown. Chantal's lips twisted into a wry smile. Another big winner. Her restless gaze drifted to the face of the man standing next to the woman. He wasn't smiling, but there was unabashed pleasure on his face. As if drawn by her gaze, he glanced up and saw Chantal staring at him.

Unable to withstand the intensity in his eyes, she turned away, aware that her heart had kicked into a faster rhythm. The stranger's face was becoming familiar. He'd graced Rambler's with his presence last night and the night before. Come to think of it, he'd been there every night since she'd arrived.

There was no denying that he was a handsome devil, though he wasn't the type to catch her eye. She liked men with smooth good looks and elegant, whipcord bodies. This man was just over average height and looked like a cross between Steven Seagal and a lineman for the New Orleans Saints. Though it was the height of style and fit his broad shoulders to perfection, his elegant black tuxedo looked out of place on a man whose Roman nose had obviously been broken at least once, a man who looked as if he'd be much more comfortable in a pair of worn jeans and battered sneakers.

His hair was nice and thick, she thought. A rich chocolate brown. Slightly curly, it was cut short and brushed to the side. Recalcitrant strands defied style and fell onto his furrowed forehead. His eyebrows were heavy, shielding eyes of an indeterminable color. It was obvious that he'd shaved, but the firm line of his jaw already sported a bluish shadow. His bottom lip was full; his upper had a flaring, Sean Connery bow at the outer edges. It was the kind of hard, sexy mouth that didn't smile much, the kind that inspired dangerous fantasies, the kind designed to drive a woman crazy with wanting....

"Hello, gorgeous."

The soft salutation scattered her thoughts. She turned to see another darkly handsome man standing before her, a smile lifting the corners of a very black, very luxuriant, mustache.

Nick Balodinas, another frequent visitor to the casino, was a wealthy Greek in the States on business. Charming to the extreme and oozing confidence, he'd sweet-talked her into going to dinner with him the night before. A dinner date had been a welcome change. The advances that followed, weren't.

Chantal raised her chin a trifle and met his dancing gaze with a frigid look. "Hello, Nick. Goodbye, Nick." She turned to walk away.

"Obviously, you still haven't forgiven me."

Chantal turned, a quizzical expression on her face. "For what?"

He reached out and brushed back a lock of thick chestnut hair. She jerked away from his touch.

"You know for what," he said softly. "For kissing you, trying to...touch you. I've said I'm sorry. You know I'd never want to upset you."

Chantal's lips quirked in a humorless smile. "Obviously, Nick, you've mistaken me for someone who gives a damn."

Again, she turned to leave. She'd gone no more than two steps when she felt his fingers curl around her upper arm. She glared up at him from over her shoulder. "Let go."

"Not until you agree to give me another chance."

"Back off, buddy."

Nick's grip loosened in a natural reflex action to the terse command. Both Chantal and the Greek turned. Her breath caught when she saw that her rescuer was none other than the unknown man she'd been thinking about before Nick began harassing her. The stranger was even better-looking than she'd thought—in a rough, exciting sort of way.

Nick drew himself to his full height, which was a half a head taller than the stranger's. "This is between me and the lady," he snapped. "It's none of your business."

The stranger's midnight-dark eyes bored into Nick's. "Since it doesn't look like the lady is interested, I'm making it my business."

Long seconds ticked by as the two men stood almost nose to nose, their hands curled into loose fists. There was something about the newcomer that Chantal found intimidating. Something about the way he carried himself hinted of power and temper kept under tight rein. Her nails cut half moons in her palms as she vacillated between going and getting security and trying to guess which one would throw the first punch.

Just when the tension reached almost unbearable proportions, Nick took a step backward and held up both hands, palms out. "All right," he said. "You win."

The emotion in the stranger's smile was hard to place, something between world weary and cocky. His massive shoulders lifted in a shrug. "What can I say?"

Nick turned to Chantal. "I beg your pardon. I never meant to cause you any grief." She watched him walk away and turned back to her rescuer, a look of gratitude in her eyes.

"Thank you, Mr. . . . ."

"Garvey," he said, all vestige of threat gone. He held out a strong hand with a fine sprinkling of dark hair on the back. His warm fingers closed around hers. "Dylan Garvey. And it was my pleasure, Ms. . . . ."

"Robichaux. Chantal."

"Chantal." The name rolled off his tongue like a caress. "Sounds exotic, elegant . . . sexy—like you."

Chantal's wary heart missed a beat. She forced her gaze to his. The directness in his eyes caught her off guard. "Is this a come-on, Mr. Garvey?" she asked, appalled at the hint of breathlessness she heard in her voice.

"And if it is?"

"I'd advise you not to waste your time."

"Is that advice or a warning?" he asked.

There was unabashed defiance in the tilt of her chin. "However you want to take it."

His massive shoulders lifted in a careless shrug; his eyes never left hers. "It's my time."

Chantal wasn't sure how to handle his directness. She was used to innuendo, games. Dylan Garvey seemed determined to go straight to the heart of things, an approach she found refreshing and frightening.

"So how did you come by the name Chantal?" he asked, surprising her with the sudden, unexpected question.

Chantal's creamy shoulders, bared by the teal moiré dress she wore, moved in a slight shrug. "My mother gave her daughters French names. She was an incurable romantic, but for the life of me, I don't know why."

His eyebrows climbed in question. "Is that a trace of cynicism I hear?"

"Oh, it's more than a trace, Mr. Garvey."

"I take it you don't believe in white knights, romance and fairy-tale endings?"

"White knights went out with the whalebone corsets," she said. "In most cases, romance is confused with sex, and fairy-tale endings are as rare as a flawless diamond. I guess you could say that my own experiences have made me a skeptic. The only person I know I can count on is me." It was a lie, she knew she could count on her family, but something inside her warned that this man was dangerous. Maybe her callous attitude would turn him off.

Instead, one corner of his mouth crawled upward in a humorless half smile. "Ah, a woman after my own heart. Tell me more."

"Why should I?"

"Because I'm bored?" he queried, taking her arm in a firm but gentle grip. Against her better judgment, Chantal allowed him to guide her through the crowd to a semisecluded spot near the exit.

"I've seen you here every night," he observed, "but I never see you gambling. Do you work here?"

"Temporarily," she said, still wary of his persistence. "The Ramblers are my sister-in-law's parents, and they needed someone to oversee the place for a few weeks while they vacationed in Europe. You might say I'm here under duress."

He still didn't smile, but there was a twinkle in his darker-than-sin eyes. "Another victim of the old guilt trip."

Despite herself, Chantal found her lips curving in response. Dylan Garvey was a hard man to resist. "A victim of a smooth-talker—my sister-in-law. She could talk Eskimos into air-conditioning with that slow Tennessee drawl of hers."

He laughed then, an unexpectedly rich, warm sound that lapped onto the shore of Chantal's senses like waves of warm honey. The man was trouble, she thought again, struggling to still the rapid beating of her heart. He was too intense, too unpredictable. *Too darn sexy*. And she was too vulnerable. Why else would she be talking to him so freely? It wasn't like her at all.

"Where's home?" he asked. "I hear an unmistakable accent, but I can't quite place it."

"Louisiana. Thibodaux. What about you?"

"Chicago."

"I didn't think you sounded like a local," she observed.

"So," he said, changing the topic again, "how long are you going to be in our fair city?"

"Five more weeks, two days and—" she glanced at the plain watch circling her small wrist "—approximately twelve-and-a-half hours. Not that I'm count-ing."

"You don't like Jersey?"

She shook her head. "I'm a country girl. Popula-tions over twenty or thirty thousand make me real nervous. And running a casino is certainly different from managing a hotel."

"Is that what you do back in Tiba . . . ?"

"Thibodaux," she supplied. "It's what I did until the place I worked for went bankrupt. What about you? What do you do?"

"I'm in sales," he supplied smoothly.

Chantal's disbelief was obvious. "You don't look like a salesman."

His mouth twisted into another of those supposed-to-be smiles. "I sell workout equipment to health clubs."

"Oh." Not that she was any judge, but if Dylan Garvey's physique was any indication, he looked like a man who used the workout equipment, not one who sold it.

Across the way, the redhead squealed again. Real-ity and sanity returned with a vengeance; the easy rapport that bound her to Dylan Garvey vanished. Even though her disappointment was sharp and un-expected, Chantal couldn't help sighing with relief. She was far too drawn to the challenging directness in Dylan Garvey's eyes and to his devastating, but rare, smile. She needed some time to bolster her defenses.

"Your friend is having a good night," she said pointedly.

Dylan glanced over his shoulder at the woman, and then met Chantal's accusatory gaze with more of that disconcerting directness. "Some people are lucky, some aren't."

And she was one of the ones who weren't, she reminded herself. Pride lent an edge to her voice. "If you'll excuse me, I have some things to do in the office." She held out her hand. "Thanks again for your help."

If Dylan Garvey was offended or surprised by her sudden shift in attitude, it didn't show. He shook her hand with a firm grip. "Sure. Catch you later."

Chantal left him standing there and headed for Lyle Kennedy's office, where she spent the next hour trying to put the encounter and the man out of her mind. But when Lyle arrived at midnight and Chantal went upstairs to Jon and Ellen Rambler's apartment where she was staying, she couldn't help noticing that Dylan Garvey and his buxom redhead were still trying their luck.

She showered and washed her hair to rid herself of the smell of smoke and the tensions of the evening; then, donning a faded T-shirt she'd talked Cade out of, she climbed into bed. Closing her eyes, she willed herself to sleep, but instead of rest, a montage of Dylan Garvey memories flitted through her mind—his rough good looks, his gestures, his slow seductive smile. Lord, that smile! He ought to have a warning tattooed on his forehead: Caution. This Smile May Be Hazardous to Your Heart.

Which brought up a very unsettling thought. Why, after so many months of disinterest in men, had she found one who made her pulse race? More important, what was it about Dylan that made her pulse race when he wasn't her type at all?

It's the old hormones, Chantal. It's been too long, that's all. Irritated by the thought, she flopped onto her back and flung her forearm across her eyes. But even with her eyes closed and covered she'd still been able to see the white flash of teeth in his dark face and the way his eyes crinkled at the corners. . . .

"Ms. Robichaux? Are you awake?"

The softly voiced question brought Chantal's thoughts back to the present. She recognized the woman in the doorway as the same nurse who'd brought the baby in to her earlier. Melanie something or other. "Come on in," she said, "I'm awake."

"I've come to get the baby. It's time for a feeding, and I figured you could use a little rest by now."

"Sorry. You just missed him," Chantal said with a smile. "Somebody came and got him a little while ago."

"How long ago was that?"

The nurse's frowning countenance sent a tremor of unease rippling down Chantal's spine. She glanced at the clock on the far wall. "About twenty minutes ago. Is something wrong?"

The woman offered what Chantal surmised was supposed to be an encouraging smile. Somehow it failed to reassure. "Oh, no. I'm sure it's just a mix-up on the duty roster. I'll go double check."

The nurse was at the door when Chantal called "Wait!" The LPN turned. "It was Ann Gordon who came and got the baby."

"Ann Gordon?"

"That's what her name tag said."

"What did she look like?"

"A little overweight. Short brown hair. Glasses."

The smile the nurse urged to her lips didn't quite reach her eyes. She winked. "I'll be right back."

Chantal felt the muscles in her shoulders tighten and told herself to relax. It was amazing how fast she'd fallen into the worrying mother mode. She was wringing her hands when the LPN returned with a co-worker.

The forty-something woman neared Chantal's bed with an embarrassed smile that was at odds with the anxiety mirrored in her brown eyes. Something deep inside Chantal—a mother's instinct?—told her that something was very wrong.

"Hi. I'm Pat Mullins, the floor supervisor. It seems we've got our wires crossed somehow."

Chantal's eyes widened in sudden apprehension. "What do you mean?"

Pat Mullins's smile looked strained. "We seem to have misplaced your baby."

"What!" Chantal cried, trying to push herself into a sitting position in spite of the pain in her abdomen.

She felt Pat's hands, gentle and surprisingly strong, press against her shoulders. "Just relax, Chantal. It's going to be all right."

Her low monotone was somewhat soothing. Chantal stopped struggling. Her worried gaze moved from the supervisor to the other nurse, who refused to look at her.

"What's happened to my baby?" Chantal asked. Her voice trembled, and tears spilled down her cheeks.

Pat Mullins clasped her hand. "If you can just answer a few questions, I'm sure we can get this cleared up in no time."

Chantal swallowed back her misery, swiped at her tears and nodded.

"What time did you say the nurse came and got your baby?"

"About twenty-five minutes ago now," Chantal said, looking at the clock again.

"Are you sure?"

"Positive." Chantal's voice was husky with emotion. "It was about the time my brother and his wife left."

Pat Mullins looked at the LPN. "Right smack-dab in the middle of shift change."

The other nurse, Melanie Pierce, nodded, as if she understood some unspoken comment.

"You said her name was Ann Gordon, that she was plump, wore glasses and had short brown hair, right?"

Chantal nodded.

"Did she say why she'd come for him?" Pat Mullins asked.

"She said the pediatrician was here and wanted to circumcise him."

"Pediatrician?" Melanie Pierce blurted, speaking for the first time. "Pediatricians don't—"

Pat Mullins shot her co-worker a quelling glance and directed her attention back to Chantal. "Who is your pediatrician?"

"Dr. Fontaine."

The supervisor turned to the LPN. "You stay with her while I go check it out."

"But—"

"I know, Melanie," Pat Mullins said, the sharpness in her voice unmistakable, "but I need to make sure." She left the room. The minutes ticked by, one slow second followed by another. Chantal wanted to ask Melanie Pierce what the supervisor was checking, but she was afraid she might not want to hear the answer. *Oh, Baby, where are you?*

The supervisor reappeared in a matter of minutes, a haggard look on her face.

"Well?" Chantal demanded. "Did Dr. Fontaine do the circumcision or not?"

The nurse approached the bed. "No."

The implication sank in slowly. "If he didn't send for the baby, then where did the nurse take him?"

"There's no one on staff named Ann Gordon," Pat Mullins said.

Fear stabbed Chantal's heart, then the truth hit her with the force of Hurricane Andrew, sweeping through her mind, tumbling thoughts and sensations one over the other, like so much debris, leaving nothing but barrenness in its wake. She blinked, unable to believe what her mind and her heart were telling her.

She gave a high keening wail, and in spite of the agony in her abdomen, she tried again to get up out of the bed. Melanie Pierce reached her other side in an instant, forcing her, with Pat Mullins's help, to lie back, telling her to keep still or she'd hurt herself.

"I don't care!" Chantal cried, struggling against her captors while tears streamed down her pale cheeks and harsh sobs tore at her throat. "I don't want to lie still. I want my baby, damn you!"

She didn't know how many times she screamed out her lament before they gave her a sedative and darkness began to tow her under. Her last thought before the lights went completely out was that she hadn't even had a chance to name him yet.

Chapter Two

Chantal opened her bleary eyes to discomfort and a feeling of disorientation. Darkness was encroaching on the day. All that kept the shadows at bay was the soft luminescence of a small light over the sink tucked into an alcove of her room... her room at the hospital. She glanced at the clock. Seven-thirty. She had slept away the afternoon. It was eight hours since Shiloh and Cade left.

Memory came rushing back, wiping away the last vestige of grogginess. She was in pain because she'd had a C section. She'd had a baby. A precious baby boy.

And someone had stolen him.

The feeling of panic and pain that had ripped through her earlier, making her wild and out of control, was gone. In its place was helplessness, hopelessness and a soul-deep grief that pulsed through her with every painful beat of her heart. A single sob escaped her; a solitary tear slipped down her cheek. Why had Ann Gordon taken her baby?

All she'd ever wanted was a whole family. A husband who loved her as much as she loved him, children, a nice house in the country where a puppy could romp and there was room enough for a pony. In an era where everyone wanted to be instant millionaires and to control huge corporations or to run for president, it didn't seem like such an outrageous goal, yet she was denied it at every turn.

There was a soft click and swish that signaled the opening of her door. Cade stepped inside, a cup of vending machine coffee in his hand. He glanced toward the bed and, seeing she was awake, smiled.

"Hi."

"Hi," she croaked through her aching throat.

"Are you okay?"

She shook her head and passed her dry tongue over her drier lips. "I don't know. I guess they told you." It was more question than statement.

Cade drew a chair closer to the bed and sat down next to her. "We were barely home when the hospital called. I came right back."

"You shouldn't have bothered. Shiloh will think I'm a nut case."

He took her hand in his, lacing their fingers together. "Shiloh loves you, and why shouldn't I have come? You're my sister. You're hurting. You'd do it for me, wouldn't you?"

Pain clawed its way up from Chantal's broken heart and lodged in her throat, bringing tears to her eyes and huskiness to her voice. "You know I would."

His hold on her hand tightened. "I thought so."

Through an enormous inner struggle, Chantal retained temporary custody of her tears. "May I have a drink?" she asked. "My mouth is so dry."

"Sure." Cade elevated the head of her bed and gave her a sip of water. They both knew they were busying themselves with the mundane to take their minds off the problem at hand. "You missed dinner, but I can probably get them to rustle you up Jell-O or something."

The thought of eating made Chantal's empty stomach churn. "I'm not hungry." Without warning, the tears she'd tried so hard to control spilled from her hazel eyes and trickled down her pale cheeks. "Oh, Cade," she cried in a soft voice, "why would anyone want to take my baby?"

"I don't know, sis," he said, regret and sorrow lacing his voice. Her handed her a tissue. "Probably because she wants one of her own. Don't worry. We'll find him. The police are already working on it."

Her eyes grew wide with surprise and disbelief. "Police!"

Cade gave her hand a comforting squeeze. "They consider it a kidnapping. I spoke with the detective in charge earlier, and they're going to want to talk to you tomorrow as soon as you're up to it."

"I don't know anything except what I've already told the nurses."

"I know, but the authorities want to hear it from you. I think they plan to get a description from you and do a composite drawing of the woman for the newspaper.''

Chantal's fingers made a tight fist around the crumpled tissue. The magnitude of what was happening was daunting... frightening. She remembered all the times she'd watched stories about child abductions on the news and on other television programs. She couldn't recall the success rate of finding those lost children, but she had a gut feeling that it wasn't terrific. She drew a shaky breath and looked askance at him. ''Do you really think they'll find her?''

''Of course I do.''

They sat in silence, each lost in the quagmire of their own thoughts and fears. Cade took a sip of his cooling coffee.

''Chantal, I want to say something, and you aren't going to like it.'' The determination in his voice demanded her full attention. ''I know you've been dead set against telling Dylan about the baby, but under the circumstances, I don't think you have any choice. It's his son who's missing, too.''

She hadn't thought of it in that way. When she'd first learned she was pregnant, she'd tried to put herself in Dylan's shoes to see if she could figure out how he'd feel. She'd always come to the decision that it would be best if he didn't know. But Cade had a valid point. This was different. If something happened, if— God forbid—they never got the baby back, how could she live with herself, knowing that Dylan hadn't even known of his son's existence?

Her fingers plucked nervously at the sheet. ''You're probably right, but I hate to think what he'll say.''

"I imagine he'll be furious," Cade, who was never one to spare the truth, said in his usual blunt way. "But he'll get over it."

"What if he doesn't care?"

"C'mon, sis. I can't imagine you falling for anyone that insensitive."

Dylan, insensitive? No. But he wasn't a gentle, tender sort of man, either. He was bold—brash, even. A man with a take-charge attitude and a wellspring of energy that made her feel as if she was swimming in molasses most of the time. But that wasn't why she feared contacting him. The real reason went much deeper.

"What if he tries to take the baby away from me?"

Cade offered her a crooked smile. "It'll never happen. The worst possible scenario is that some judge might grant joint custody."

She scraped the tangled hair away from her face. "I suppose you're right."

"There's something else you should consider, here."

"What?" Her eyes held a question.

"Dylan is a cop. He might be able to help in the search."

That hadn't occurred to Chantal, either, but it was certainly something to consider.

"At least give it some thought." Cade rose, tossed his empty cup into a nearby trash can and gave a mighty stretch.

Chantal smiled at him. He was more than all right for a brother. "I will," she said. "In the meantime I want you to go home. You're tired. I promise not to go off the deep end again. And I'm sure not going to crawl out of this bed and track down the woman myself. It hurts too darn much."

He grinned. "Sure?"

"Positive." Her voice grew soft with love and concern. "Go home, big brother. I'm fine."

Cade looked at her carefully. Satisfied that she was in control of her fears, he nodded. "Okay, I will, but I'll be back first thing in the morning."

"I'll be right here."

He brushed a kiss to her forehead, told her goodnight and left her alone with her fears and her memories. Chantal lowered her bed back down and threw a forearm over her face, trying to dredge up the courage to make the call. Cade was right. Dylan would be furious. She'd get no sympathy from him. Everything about Dylan Garvey was hard: his perfectly shaped mouth that could drive a woman to a delicious insanity, his body... his heart.

By the time she realized she was pregnant, she'd gotten over her misplaced anger about his lying about his job. Time had put things in perspective. Common sense told her that his telling her he was a salesman was just part of being an undercover cop, but her past heartaches and disappointments in love made her wonder if his job description also included her seduction. Had he considered his pursuit of her a fringe benefit, a means of passing the time while he tried to catch the person responsible for the thefts at the casino?

Despite what Cade thought, she'd given careful consideration to telling Dylan about the baby. As hard as she'd tried, she could never form a clear picture of how he would react at learning she was having his child. She couldn't imagine him cuddling an infant, changing a diaper, mopping milk off his shirt. He was too rugged, too masculine, too... hard. So, she'd decided against telling him. She would face the future alone, just as she had the better part of her life.

Though she had spent her pregnancy alone and lonely, she couldn't place all the blame for what had happened on Dylan's shoulders. She had accepted her part in the fiasco, even though it wasn't like her to fall for a man so fast. One-night stands and casual sex weren't her style. She supposed she could attribute the first time they'd made love to the fact that she'd been held at gunpoint during a robbery and was eager to celebrate life, but that didn't explain or excuse what happened between them the following day. Dylan had given her ample time to back out, plenty of opportunities to say no.

A shiver rippled through her at the memory of his hard-muscled body, slick with sweat, moving over hers, stoking the fires of her desire with each masterful thrust, taking her to the edge of ecstasy and beyond....

In retrospect, she could see that saying no to him had been impossible, even though there was never any mention of his heart being involved. She was too needy. Too hungry for what he offered. And though he had murmured hungry sex words in her ear, had worshipped her body with near reverence, he hadn't said a thing about commitment or love.

At the time, she'd been so caught up in the moment that she hadn't been able to think beyond the next kiss, the next caress. She hadn't cared about the consequences of the night or where tomorrow might lead.

When she was able to consider it rationally, she realized that there was little chance of it becoming anything more. When she returned to Louisiana, she would never see him again.

Then she'd found out she was pregnant. They'd been careful, or so she'd thought. She remembered Dylan's curse, his profuse apology for the breaking of the condom, his assuring her that it was okay, he was okay.

Pregnancy had been her last concern. She shouldn't have been ovulating, but the bout of flu she'd suffered that month must have messed up her cycle. She'd been angry at first—at Dylan, at herself, at fate—but once she'd gotten used to the idea, she'd been thrilled.

At first she worried about what her family and the rest of the world would think. As usual, they came through for her, especially Cade. Her brother was a realist. He assured her that her pregnancy was meant to be and stood behind her decision to have the baby. But even he hadn't been able to talk her into telling Dylan.

Now it looked as if she'd be telling him after all, and the prospect frightened her. She hated exposing her vulnerability to anyone, especially a man with so much power to hurt her.

Time away from those two days' indiscretion had given her a much-needed objectivity, and she could now see that her reluctance to confide in him was based on more than fear that he'd be angry. Now she could admit that during the month she'd known him, she'd come to care about him more than she let on— to him or herself. She could admit that while his utter masculinity and the aura of danger he projected was frightening on an intellectual level, it also made her feel safe somehow, as if he could slay any dragons that came after her, rescue her from any dangers that might lay ahead.

Somehow, since leaving Atlantic City, her heart had come to realize that Dylan wasn't the kind of person who would hurt someone else without just cause. It also told her that if she was truthful about her reasons for not telling him about the baby, she'd admit that as much as she feared he might try to take the baby away from her, she was more afraid he would recognize the tender feelings for him that were growing inside her at an alarming rate.

It was amazing how she'd refused to see the truth. There had been plenty of clues, both about who and what Dylan was and about how she felt about him, but she hadn't picked up on them. Or if she had, she had pushed those clues aside.... Her thoughts drifted back again....

Chantal's gaze volleyed from the noisy crowd to the elegant marble-and-brass entry of Rambler's. She hadn't seen Dylan in days. If he'd been at the casino, he must have come during Lyle Kennedy's shift—not that it mattered, she hastened to assure herself. She moved through the throng, her senses awash in the cloying scent of a hundred mingling perfumes, the crush of too many people in too small a space, the sound of voices raised in jubilation and despair. She was nearing the office when someone bumped into her from behind. She saw a masculine arm reach out, felt herself pulled against a masculine body, felt a hand deliberately cover her breast.

Shock rendered her speechless. She struggled to regain her balance at the same time she tried to move out of the man's reach. Then she felt another hand grip her arm, and miraculously the man was gone. Breathless, confused, Chantal turned to see what was happening.

Dylan stood a few feet away, a scowl furrowing his forehead and his mouth compressed into a straight, uncompromising line. He was gripping the upper arm of a lanky man whose back was literally against a wall. The stranger, who looked as if he'd had more than a few too many free drinks, was sobering rapidly at the menace that radiated from every pore of Dylan's body.

"Look, mister, I'm s-sorry," he stammered.

Dylan released his hold on the man's shirtfront and smoothed it with exaggerated care. "Just watch where you're going and who you're feeling up, buddy." The man gave a vehement nod, edged around Dylan and disappeared into the crowd.

A ripple of unease shivered through Chantal. Why had Dylan reacted so violently? She didn't particularly like being grabbed by a stranger, but Dylan's reaction had been a trifle too strong—hadn't it?

While she was trying to make sense of the situation, he turned and took a step toward her. She recoiled an involuntary step. Even as she did, she saw that she had misjudged him. There was nothing but concern on his face, an emotion that, when he saw her reaction, was replaced with a polite mien that bordered on blankness. Without a word, he too disappeared into the milling, intense crowd.

He came to the casino every night following the incident, the redhead clinging to his arm. Not once during that long week had he made an effort to strike up a conversation with her. Chantal told herself she wasn't jealous; she told herself that his girlfriend probably wouldn't like it if he spent time with someone else; she told herself the woman seemed far more interested in gambling than she was in Dylan. It didn't make sense, but then, nothing had made much sense since she'd met Dylan Garvey, least of all her preoccupation with him.

To make things worse, two more pieces of jewelry had come up missing, and Chantal and Lyle were forced to deal with the irate customers and the police. The whole situation made her furious. More than once, she found herself thinking that if Jeremy hadn't been such a slime, she'd be at home nights cooking dinner and wrangling a couple of kids instead of being hundreds of miles from her family running a darned gambling casino and worrying about jewelry being heisted! Life wasn't fair. But then, she'd learned that lesson when she was eight and her dad had walked out on them.

On Thursday night, Dylan arrived alone. From her place across the room, Chantal took the opportunity to study him at leisure. After more than a week of missing him, she had passed the point of rationalizing or denying her relief to see that he was by himself, just as she no longer tried to deny her unwanted attraction to him.

Even from her vantage point, she could tell that he looked as alone and lonely as she felt. The questions she'd nurtured so carefully the past few days vanished like a fistful of coins at the slot machines. New ones took their place. What was he thinking? she wondered. What was bothering him? What caused those lightning mood changes? Who the heck was Dylan Garvey, anyway—the sexy rough-around-the-edges salesman with the flirty manner or the tough guy who made people back away in fear?

It was nearing midnight when he finally looked up and saw her. For long seconds, neither looked away. Chantal couldn't have broken the eye contact if she'd wanted to. And she didn't. When he rose and started toward her, her heart jerked into a ragged rhythm.

Get a grip! she chastised herself. *You aren't some sex-starved teen. So the man is handsome, and he's lonely. So are several million other men in the world.*

But several million other men didn't have that intense way of looking at her—as if he'd like to snatch her up and carry her off somewhere to do deliciously naughty things to her.

He came to a stop a few feet away. "Hey," he said, no smile on the horizon.

"Hi." She hoped she didn't sound as nervous, as gauche, as she felt.

"Are you still counting the days?"

"I beg your pardon?"

"Last week you were counting the days until the Ramblers got back."

"Oh, that." She shook her head and brushed back a tendril of hair that had escaped the sleek knot atop her head. "I have about a month left."

"Maybe I can talk you into coming over to my place for dinner one night before you go back home," he said, his eyes caressing her bare shoulders and the swell of her breasts in the gold bustier she wore with sleek black velvet pants.

How had the conversation turned from pleasantries to personal so quickly? Chantal kept her gaze glued to the pristine whiteness of his pleated shirtfront, afraid to succumb to the raw need in his eyes. Giving in would only lead to a heartache she was ill-equipped to handle. "I don't think that would be a good idea."

"Which? Having dinner with me, or having dinner at my apartment?"

Deliberately, because she knew she had to, she raised her gaze to his. "Either."

Twin slashes appeared between his eyebrows. "Why?"

"Because you frighten me."

Other than a glimmer of surprise in his eyes, Dylan's expression never changed. "I frighten you? Why?"

"I saw you scare a man sober the other night."

"I didn't touch the bum."

"I know. Scary, isn't it?"

Instead of the apology she half expected, he shrugged. "I guess I'm just an intimidating sort of guy."

Frowning, she gave a slow nod. "I guess you are. Was it necessary to be so rough?"

His eyebrows snapped into another frown. His voice held irritation. "You haven't seen rough, lady. He had his hands all over you."

"He was drunk. He lost his balance."

"And grabbed a handful of you to steady himself," he said, his voice vibrating with remembered anger. "Does drunk make it okay to feel you up?" He ignored her gasp at his deliberate crudeness and continued, "If it does, I'll keep it in mind."

"He didn't know what he was doing," she maintained, her own irritation on the rise.

"Like hell. You're a gorgeous woman, Ms. Robichaux. Just looking at you in that get-up is enough to give a man a har—" he paused, aware that he was about to say something he shouldn't "—heart attack."

Chantal wasn't fooled. Hot color stole into her cheeks.

"Besides, I thought he was—" Dylan broke off in midsentence and plunged his hands into his slacks pockets. "Never mind. It's complicated. But I still think the jerk had it coming."

"And that makes it okay, I guess," she said in total disbelief. "The workings of the male mind never cease to amaze me," she said, turning to walk away.

He reached out and grasped her arm. "Chantal."

The sound of him speaking her name halted her retreat as effectively as his hold on her. She couldn't remember ever hearing him say her name. Turning, she saw a hint of anger in his dark eyes, but she had the feeling the emotion was directed at himself.

"You're a cold, hard man."

"So they say." The impatience in his voice was at odds with the gentle way his thumb caressed her bare arm. "I'm sorry for upsetting you. I'm sorry for whatever the hell you want me to be sorry for. Look, I'm not asking for a lifetime commitment. Just dinner. If it's any consolation, I've never hurt anyone without just cause before."

"I know." And somehow, she did.

"Then what's the problem?"

"There's no sense starting something when I'll be leaving in a month," she said.

He mulled that over for a moment. His lips quirked up at the corner in a passable rendition of a smile. "Starting something. Does that mean you're attracted to me?"

"I don't want to be," she said with disarming honesty.

"But if you ignore it—and me—it'll go away, is that it?"

She shrugged her shapely shoulders. "Something like that."

"Hell, I never knew it was that easy." He shook his head in disbelief. "I'm sorry, but I can't buy all this. I don't think for one minute it's as easy for you to control your feelings as you'd like me to believe. What about love?"

"It's a luxury I haven't allowed myself in a long time."

"You haven't *allowed* yourself?"

Dylan laughed, a response as rare as his smiles. The rich throaty sound would have been attractive if it weren't tinged with bitterness. He released her arm and captured her rounded chin between his thumb and fingers. She wanted to pull free, wanted to tell him to give her some space. Wanted to lean closer and see if the promise of his lips was all she imagined it would be. But all she did was look up at him with wide, questioning eyes.

He shook his head. "Don't you ever get cold and lonely up there?" he murmured, his breath a sweet vapor against her lips.

Chantal could hardly hear the soft-spoken question over the wild pounding of her heart. "Up where?"

"In that damned ivory tower you've locked yourself in."

"I'm not—" she began, but his lips stopped her denial. Warm and hungry and demanding, his mouth claimed hers in a kiss that sent her senses soaring and her spirits plummeting. It was everything she'd dreamed it would be. Everything she'd prayed it wouldn't. It was heaven. It was hell. Filled with sweet promises and hints of heartbreak. And over almost as soon as it was begun.

Chantal struggled to lift her eyelashes. The look in his eyes was as hot and steamy as August in Louisiana. He wiped the moisture from his lips with the back of his hand, as if to erase all traces of the kiss. "The feeling's mutual."

"What feeling?"

"You scare me, too, lady. You scare me real bad." And with that, he turned and walked away.

The following night, Chantal was dreaming about missing diamond necklaces and thieves who looked like her ex-husband when a persistent buzzing roused her from a restless sleep. Disoriented, she looked around for the source of the annoying sound and realized that it was pitch dark. It took another few seconds to associate the buzzing with the doorbell. Rubbing her eyes, she glanced at the bedside clock. It was just past 3:00 a.m. Who on earth could be at her door at three in the morning?

She debated whether or not to acknowledge the summons, but another impatient buzz sent her scrambling for her robe. It was obvious that if she didn't see who it was, she wouldn't get any relief.

"Who's there?" she called.

"Chantal?"

The voice was low and masculine, but she couldn't place it. Rising up on tiptoe, she pressed her eye to the peek hole. Dylan. Her heartbeats went into double time.

"Chantal, are you there? Are you 'sleep?"

The slurred, almost unintelligible words and the fact that his question made no sense tipped her off that he was drunk. Or so close it didn't matter. She pressed her cheek to the door. "I *was* asleep," she said, letting the irritation she felt seep into her voice.

"You're mad. Don' be mad, baby. I've had one hell of a day fightin' the dragons, an' the fair lady's still in her iv'ry tower."

Though she had no idea what he was talking about, Chantal knew *who* he was talking about. She was the lady in the ivory tower.

"Can I come in?"

She closed her eyes and tried not to let the underlying pain in his plea prey on her common sense. She hardly knew the man. He might be dangerous. He might be a thief—or worse. "I don't think—" she began.

"Look," he said, a note of unutterable weariness in his voice, "I may not be the white knight, but I'm not one of the bad guys, either. I'm not a rapist or a ser'al killer. I swear."

Chantal's heart twisted in empathetic pain. "Go home, Dylan," she urged in a gentle voice. "Sleep it off."

"I don' wanna go home. Let me come in," he pleaded. "I'm tired."

The simple declaration said more than he realized. She knew he was telling the truth, but his weariness was more than physical. It was bone-deep weariness, soul-deep exhaustion, the kind that came when you had no answers, much less made any sense of the questions. Knowing that she was about to cross the river of no return, Chantal unlocked the three safety locks that would let him in.

He stood leaning against the opposite wall of the narrow hallway, his arms crossed over his wide chest. She might have terrible judgment when it came to picking men, but she'd been right about one thing. He did look good in jeans. The denim pants were tight, faded and worn in all the right places, just like the lambskin bomber jacket he wore. The black T-shirt that was tucked into the low-slung jeans hugged his chest, defining the hard musculature beneath and drawing attention to his flat stomach.

His hair looked as if he'd run his fingers through it, and if she had to guess, she'd wager he hadn't shaved since she'd seen him the day before. His dark eyes held a vulnerability that made her heart ache.

As she stood looking at him, he was busy doing the same to her, eyeing her from the top of her gleaming, tousled hair to her pink toenails. His gaze dawdled over her shoulders and legs—bared by the T-shirt and short robe she wore—and clung for heart-stopping seconds on the soft swell of her breasts.

Her body's unexpected response was as undeniable as the blatant desire in his eyes. The tips of her breasts tightened, and a ribbon of aching need began to unfurl throughout her lower body. It occurred to her that it had been a very long time since she'd felt those feelings and even longer since she'd acted on them.

He pushed away from the wall and started toward her, stopping an arm's length away. He lifted a hand as if to reach out and touch her cheek, but instead, he rammed both hands into the pockets of his jeans. "Hi."

"Hi," she replied, unsteadily.

"You're so beautiful." The compliment was unexpected. His voice was thick with drink and need, but there was no doubt that it came from the heart.

She crossed her arms over her aching breasts, unsure whether the action was meant to impede the ache or to deter his hot gaze. "Thanks, but I hardly think you're in a condition to know what you're saying."

His mouth quirked into a rueful quasi-grin, and he removed his right hand from his pocket to scrape it through his dark hair. "I'm drunk, aren't I?"

"I'm afraid so."

"Well, I think you're beautiful even when I'm sober," he said solemnly.

"Really?" The question was accompanied by a lift of her dark eyebrows and a considering nod.

"Really." He smiled then, an honest-to-goodness, devastating smile. The rare action changed his looks radically. He looked younger, less intimidating. Approachable. Adorable—if the imagination could be stretched enough to consider six feet, one-hundred-eighty pounds of raw masculinity adorable.

He stepped past her into the apartment. "You've got a real nice place," he said, turning to face her and stumbling slightly. "Oops!"

Chantal was beside him in an instant. In her haste to steady him, her arm went beneath his jacket. His went around her shoulders, and she found herself clamped to him, the side of her breast crushed against his chest, her bare thigh welded to his denim-clad leg. His body was warm and hard beneath her palm. The combined scents of stale cigarette smoke, soap and some cologne that was sharp, spicy and manly swamped her senses.

She glanced up, and before she realized what he was about, he ducked his head and took her lips with his. She was instantly aware of the scratchiness of his whiskers and the taste of his mouth—a combination of beer and breath mints.

Sweet heaven, his mouth... Like the rest of him, it was hard, yet incredibly soft. His kiss was firm, demanding. His tongue teased her with tentative forays between her parted lips before probing deep inside. She felt the power of the thrust all the way to the core of her womanhood, which was hot, melting in the heat of a growing desire.

Dylan ended the kiss, but his hand slipped up over her breast, cupping, kneading, destroying the last of her puny resistance. Chantal let her head fall forward against his chest, unable to fight him or the feelings his touch evoked... no longer sure she wanted to.

"It's okay," he said, his lips moving against her hair.

"What's okay?" she murmured.

"If I touch you. I'm drunk."

Ruefully, Chantal remembered their argument. It was obvious that he did, too. How like a man to remember just what he wanted to from a disagreement... the part that could be used against her.

"I don't feel so good."

All thoughts of kisses and caresses and where his advances might be leading, fled. Chantal tilted back her head to look at him. "You aren't going to be sick, are you?"

He shook his head, wiped an unsteady hand down his face and closed his eyes. "Just let me sit down a minute, okay?"

"Okay." She guided him in an unsteady path across the room to the navy, jade and maroon paisley sofa. Dylan placed his elbows on his knees and cradled his head in his hands. "Can I get you something?"

He turned his head and opened a bloodshot eye. "A glass of water?"

Chantal went to get the water, praying that he knew what he was talking about and that he wouldn't be sick. When she stepped through the door of the living room, his glass of water in hand, she saw that he had shed his jacket and battered shoes and was stretched out on the sofa, his brawny forearm flung over his face. Her gaze moved over his body with a hunger that shocked her. He was certainly put together well.

"Should never have married her," he said, effectively halting her perusal of his physical assets.

He was thinking of his wife. *Wife!* She'd never considered that he might be married. But surely he wouldn't have asked her to his place for dinner if he was married. *Ha!* she thought, recalling Jeremy's infidelity. Who knew what steps a man would sink to if he wanted a woman?

Remembering Jeremy's lies went a long way toward squashing the tender feelings Dylan's touch had roused in her. How could she have allowed herself to react to an advance based on nothing but physical need?

"Dylan." Her voice was firm with resolution. She'd get him up and send him on his way. She wouldn't fix dinner for him at his apartment or anywhere else. She'd be nice. She'd be firm. But this crazy attraction had to end. "Dylan," she said again.

Though it was an obvious effort, he moved his arm and opened his eyes.

"Here's your water."

"Too tired to drink it," he muttered. "I should never have married her, Chantal." He squinted up at her, as if the light was too bright for his eyes. "You ever been married?"

"Once," she admitted.

"What happened?"

"He lied to me."

"Oh." He accepted the simple statement and let his eyes drift shut again. His chest rose and fell with a deep, shuddering sigh. "I was married once, too," he said, the words a mere whisper.

Was. Resolutions aside, Chantal couldn't stop the leap of joy her heart made. It occurred to her that with her track record it was her luck to fall for a guy who was still carrying the torch for his ex. "What happened?"

His eyelids drifted to half-mast.

"What happened to your marriage?"

"Dragons got it," he said, the words low and slurred.

Dragons again. What did he mean? Before she could ask, she heard the soft sounds of his even breathing. He was asleep. Or passed out. Scarcely able to breathe for the warring tenderness and despair growing inside her, Chantal got a blanket from the hall closet and covered him with it.

For long moments, she stared down at him, wondering what had happened between him and his former wife. And what had triggered this new pain. Without thinking of what she was doing—or why— she leaned over and cradled his cheek with her hand. The roughness of his whiskers felt strangely erotic against her palm. She brushed the pad of her thumb over the fullness of his lower lip. He turned toward her touch, as if seeking her warmth or the comfort she offered.

Straightening, Chantal turned out the lamp and went back to her bedroom. Asleep or just out, he was free of the dragons for at least a few hours. Unfairly, his freedom had caused her more pain. She knew without a doubt that despite her reservations about him, despite her disappointments in the past, Dylan Garvey had made definite inroads into her heart. The realization was exciting. Frightening. But as she pressed her palms to her tender, aching breasts, she knew there was no denying that he made her feel more alive than she had felt in years.

Later, much later, she had fallen asleep, dreading, yet eager, to see what tomorrow might bring. Somehow, she was certain that one of its gifts would be heartbreak....

And she'd been right. As the country song said, Dylan was a heartache just looking for a place to happen. Even now, after not seeing him for so many months, she knew that whatever had been between them wasn't finished. She had to call him and tell him about the baby, and, for her at least, it would start it all over again.

Maybe he won't be angry. Maybe he won't come.

Sighing, she sank her teeth into her bottom lip, reached for the telephone, and got Atlantic City information. In a matter of seconds, she was listening to the ringing of the phone. Once, on the third ring, she started to hang up, but she gritted her teeth and gripped the receiver tighter. Surely, if he wasn't there, his answering machine would pick up.

"Hello."

Hearing his voice after she'd convinced herself that he wasn't there drew a small gasp of surprise. Reason fled.

"Hello." She heard the irritation creeping into his voice. "Look, if this is an obscene phone call, let's get on with it," he said. "If it's a joke, I've heard 'em all. Now state your business, or I'm gonna hang up. I'm watching a helluva good movie."

He meant it. "Dylan?" The single word was a hoarse croak.

"Yeah?" His voice held wariness. "Who the hell is this?"

Chantal passed a dry tongue over her dry lips. "Please, Dylan, don't hang up. It's Chantal."

Chapter Three

Chantal? Dylan leaped to his feet. Surprise sent his stomach dropping the way it had when he'd ridden a roller coaster as a kid; anguish compressed his heart, making him feel light-headed and a little sick. "Who?" he asked again, needing to make certain he'd heard right.

"Chantal."

He hadn't misunderstood. His heart began to beat out an excruciating cadence that thundered in his ears. Damn her! A muscle in his jaw knotted. He began to pace the room—as far as the long cord would allow and back again.

Why was she calling after so long? It had taken him months to get over the callous way she'd tossed aside what they shared because she felt he'd been dishonest with her about who he was. She hadn't considered his feelings, wouldn't listen to his reasoning. It hadn't mattered that the Atlantic City Police Department had sent him undercover to try and flush the thief who was hitting on the smaller casinos. Nothing mattered but that she was the person wronged.

He'd suspected he was falling for her while she was here; he was positive he hated her when she left. Now he wasn't sure what he felt. The sound of her voice was playing havoc with his mind, bringing back memories best forgotten, memories he'd struggled to bury under grueling hours of work.

"Dylan, are you there?"

The sound of her voice derailed the turbulent train of his thoughts. "Yeah, I'm here. What do you want?" He thought he heard a sharp intake of breath before a lengthy silence set in. "Come on, Chantal, spit it out. You've never been shy about what you had to say before."

"Honesty is important to me," she replied, telling him without words that she knew he was talking about their last conversation.

"Doing my job is dishonest?"

Her sigh filtered through the phone line. "Even if I'd known the truth about you from the start, there was no future in it . . . in us."

Dylan felt his blood pressure spiral upward. How could she be so blasé about the two incredible days they'd spent together? Possibly the most incredible days of his life?

"So why are you calling?" he said in a voice as cold as a blue norther.

"I need to—" she paused "—tell you something. Cade said I should, but I was afraid—"

"Cut to the chase, okay?" Dylan asked, but his mind was racing. What could she possibly have to say to him after so many months? Was she coming back? Had she changed her mind?

"I'm trying, but ... It's so hard...."

She stopped again, as if she was trying to gather her thoughts—or her courage. Dylan felt a perverse sense of satisfaction at the nervousness he heard in her voice. Chantal Robichaux. Ms. Independent, Ms. No-Nonsense, Ms. Tell-It-Like-It-Is-and-Damn-the-Consequences, was actually sputtering like a gauche teenager.

"I ... I had a baby yesterday evening."

Dylan felt as if the rush of words was an invisible fist that hit him squarely in the gut. He sank back down into a corner of the worn sofa, his blind gaze focused on a hunting print hanging across the room. A baby. Dear God...

"It was a boy."

Fresh pain replaced the dazed feeling. "Congratulations," he told her, the mockery in his voice evident, purposeful. "But you really didn't have to call and tell me."

"Oh, I'm making a mess of this," she wailed. "I didn't want to tell you, but Cade insisted that I tell you, and, under the circumstances, I thought—"

When her voice broke off again, Dylan jerked upright and pressed the receiver closer to his ear. Was that a sob? Was she crying? Well, it served her right for ripping out his heart by the roots.

"What circumstances?"

"The baby is yours."

They spoke simultaneously, but her statement far outweighed his question. Once again, Dylan wasn't sure he was hearing right. He'd fathered a child? Chantal's baby? His stunned surprise gave way to suspicion. What was she trying to pull here? How could he be sure the baby was his? He did some quick math and, recalling the broken condom, succumbed to the probability that she was telling the truth.

He blew out a steady stream of air and threaded his fingers through his dark hair, trying to absorb the reality of what she was saying. Deep inside, he knew he wanted to believe her. A baby. A son. He'd always wanted a child, but Carole had refused to bring a baby into the world because he was a cop. She'd refused to bring *his* baby into the world. Not only was he a poor risk, he wasn't good father material.

Now fate had given him a child when he least expected it, with a woman who obviously didn't want him. Why? The thoughts and reactions tumbled through his mind like stones in a rock polisher. If Chantal was so sure the baby was his, why hadn't she contacted him before? What did she want from him now?

"Why didn't you tell me sooner?" he demanded.

"I . . . I was afraid."

"Afraid? Afraid of what? That I wouldn't believe it was mine?"

"No," she told him honestly. "That never crossed my mind."

If nothing else, that convinced him she was telling the truth. "What, then? That I wouldn't help financially? I'm not a deadbeat. If you need money, I—"

"I don't want your money!" she cried. "I can take care of myself." He heard her utter a mild curse. "There were a lot of reasons I didn't call sooner, but there's no sense getting into all that now."

Dylan was getting more confused by the minute. He had the feeling she was dancing all around the real reason for contacting him. His irritation rose. "Then why did you call, Chantal?"

"Because you're a cop, and I thought you could help."

Like everything else she'd said, the statement made little sense, but there was a forlorn quality in her voice that tugged at the heartstrings he didn't even know he had anymore. "I'm not following you. You thought I could help with what?"

"Someone stole our baby, Dylan," she said, all pretense of control dissolving as she gulped back a harsh sob. "I need you...I need you to come and help find him."

He'd gained and lost a child in the span of thirty seconds. Dylan wasn't sure when—if ever—his emotions had taken such a roller-coaster ride. The suspicion he'd felt at learning he had a son had given way to surprise and euphoria and then to more suspicion. Now despair threatened to suck him under.

"What do you mean, someone stole him?"

"She came into my room and said the doctor wanted to circumcise him, but another nurse came and wanted him, and she wasn't really an aide, and they don't know where she's taken him." Chantal's voice grew louder, less controlled, as the garbled, disjointed story spilled from her. Dylan sensed she was approaching hysteria.

He struggled with his own escalating panic. "Simmer down," he urged in a low voice. "Come on, baby, calm down." He heard her take another deep breath and knew she was fighting for control.

"She took him, Dylan," she choked out around a sob. "She took my baby, and I have to have him back. I love him. Dear God, I love him so much."

A fleeting memory—one of his earliest—crossed his mind: a memory of getting pushed down by a neighbor kid and scraping his elbow, of crawling into his father's lap and telling him how the bigger boy was picking on him. A memory of needing love and reassurances that it would be okay, and getting scolded instead.

"Boys don't cry. Sissies cry. Now, get on down from here. It's time you learned to stand up for yourself."

Dylan wasn't on familiar terms with love, he didn't understand it, but it was something he believed in nonetheless. Not to believe would be the end of the hope that kept him going.

"Will you come?"

"You told me you didn't need me or any man," he reminded her, flinging her parting words back at her. But deep in his heart, he knew he'd go. He had to.

"I know what I said. Do you want an apology? I'm sorry. If you want me to beg, I'll get down on my hands and knees. I'll do anything you want, Dylan, but just say you'll come!" she choked out. "I need you."

Dylan shut his eyes, and he hardened his heart against the anguish in her voice. If he didn't watch out, she'd have him tied in knots again. "I'll come," he said at last, "but I'd like to point out that maybe you ought to start practicing what you preach."

"I don't know what you're talking about."

"A lie of omission is still a lie, Chantal. If that woman hadn't taken the baby, would you have told me about him?"

Her silence was answer and condemnation.

"Enough said." Before she could reply, he asked, "What hospital are you in?"

"Thibodaux General."

"I'll be there as soon as I can arrange things," he told her, and cradled the receiver before she could reply.

He let his head fall back against the sofa and stared up at the ceiling. A child. A son. Gone before he'd known of his existence. It wasn't fair, his heart cried out as he closed his burning eyes. It wasn't fair at all. He swallowed hard, gritted his teeth, clenched his fists and cursed the fates. After long moments, he reached for the phone and dialed the station.

The phone clicked in Chantal's ear and a long buzz indicated that the connection had been severed. She dashed the moisture from her eyes and cradled her own receiver. Drained, she sank back against the pillows. She'd been right about his reaction. He was angry. Furious. But he was coming to help look for the baby, and that was all that mattered. She could take his anger and his accusations as long as he helped get her son back.

At the thought of accusations, she recalled his saying she'd lied to him. She hadn't thought of her silence in that way, but she supposed it was true. She had been dishonest, and for far less reason than he had been. Was her reluctance to call him motivated by selfishness instead of fear?

She didn't know anymore. She was too emotionally wrung out to think straight. And she hurt. Even with the pain medicine, the incision from her C section throbbed like an infected tooth, and her breasts, full of the milk that the baby wasn't there to take, ached painfully. She wanted to fall asleep and wake up to find him back in the nursery, all safe and sound. She wanted to curl up in someone's arms and be told that everything was going to be all right, the way Dylan had the first time they'd made love....

Chantal was sitting in the office, the newspaper spread out on the desk, counting the minutes until Lyle arrived and she could go upstairs. She'd read her horoscope and the comic strips and was working on the crossword puzzle, but try as she might, she couldn't forget the way Dylan had kissed her at the apartment, four nights earlier. When she'd awakened the next morning, he was gone, and she hadn't seen him since.

She told herself it didn't matter, that he was nothing but another guy looking for a fleeting affair. Falling for his line would lead to nothing but trouble. The problem was that, unlike Nick Balodinas, Dylan didn't really have a line, and all her rationalizations didn't stop her growing awareness of him.

She was just picking up the discarded newsprint to give the crossword puzzle another go when she heard a shrill feminine shriek followed by a high-pitched, unintelligible exchange against the backdrop of a hundred babbling voices. These weren't the cries of excited winners. The collective voices held shock and fear and disbelief. Chantal's stomach churned, while various scenarios flashed through her mind.

Leaping to her feet, she rounded the corner of the desk and headed for the door. Running as fast as her straight satin dress and heels would allow, she burst out of the short hallway and into the casino proper. A common gasp went up from the crowd. Before she could do more than grasp the fact that all of the room's occupants seemed to be facing her, a masculine voice growled "Don't move," and a rough arm snaked out and grabbed her just beneath her breasts. She was jerked back so hard against the man's body that the air whooshed from her. Something cold and hard pressed against her temple. Instinct told her not to fight; it was a gun.

Dear God, what was happening? She didn't want to die, wasn't ready to. She hadn't lived yet. She hadn't been truly loved yet. There were so many things she hadn't experienced. . . .

Harsh breathing rasped in her ear. Her knees threatened to give way, but terror held her rigid. "Please," she said, her voice breaking. "Please don't hurt me."

"Shut up!" the voice hissed as she was half dragged toward the exit. "Just shut up!"

"Let the woman go and give yourself up," someone from the crowd called. "The place is crawling with cops."

Afraid to turn her head, Chantal cut her gaze toward the feminine voice and had the impression of red hair piled high and a revolver pointed at her and her captor.

"Put your gun away!" the man holding her shrilled in a voice that warned that he couldn't be pushed. "I'll kill her! I swear I will!"

Her heart pounding in her throat, her ears ringing with dizziness, Chantal squeezed her eyes shut as the assailant maneuvered them toward the door. If he planned to kill her, she didn't want to see it coming. A picture of Dylan flashed through her mind. Dylan making Nick Balodinas back down; Dylan scaring a man sober. Dylan, a man whose very presence was intimidating. Where was he when she needed him? *Please, please.* It was a plea and a prayer.

"Hey! What's going on?" The query came from behind them, near the double entry doors. Someone coming to gamble and walking into a nightmare...

"Get the hell out of here!" the man yelled.

Chantal felt the absence of pressure at her temple and heard two shots ring out. She gave a sharp cry and prayed that they were a warning. Tears of terror squeezed out from beneath her eyelids. She drew in a shallow breath, and the scent of gunpowder assaulted her nostrils. Then the gun was back at her temple again. The barrel was hot against her flesh.

She heard a muffled thud—the double doors closing behind them? The fresh scent of out-of-doors and the fumes of car exhaust assailed her olfactory senses. She heard the sharp disbelieving cries of people on the sidewalk. Unexpectedly, the man halted dead in his tracks, and she felt his body stiffen.

"How does it feel to have a gun pointed at your head, dirtbag—huh?"

Chantal's eyes flew open. The voice, which came from behind her captor, wasn't familiar, but it held the same unmistakable note of command she'd heard in Dylan's voice the night he'd slammed the drunk against the wall.

"Come on, buddy. Let her go," the voice continued in a pleasant, conversational tone, "or I'll blow your friggin' brains out."

"No way. You back off or I'll kill her," Chantal's captor commanded. "I swear it." There was a quaver in his voice that his forced bravado couldn't hide.

"You kill her, man, and there are half a dozen cops who'll empty their pieces into you." The statement was delivered in a chilling, emotionless voice. "Come on, pal, make it easy on yourself and let her go."

Chantal felt the tightness of her captor's grip loosen the slightest bit. From the corner of her eye, she saw his gun lower. After that, things happened so quickly she couldn't separate them. All she knew was that she was wrenched free suddenly. Her legs gave way, and a woman wearing a cop's uniform reached out to steady her.

"Come on, honey," the policewoman said. "Let's go inside and get something hot to drink."

As they made their way to the door, Chantal saw the man. He was wearing an expensive suit and looked to be in his mid-forties. Arms and legs spread wide, he embraced the side of the casino while another cop patted him down. He didn't even look at her as she passed. She suppressed a shiver and looked away with a prayer of thanksgiving.

Upstairs, in the Ramblers' apartment, Chantal answered some questions posed by the policewoman, who thanked her, told her to take it easy and left. It wasn't until Chantal had stripped out of her satin dress and stood beneath the stinging spray of a scalding shower that the full impact of what she'd survived hit her, leaving her weak with relief and scared to the marrow. With the hot water beating down on her bent head, she began to cry—slow, silent tears that mingled with the water streaming over her face and body.

She wasn't sure how long she cried, but her tears and the hot water ran out at approximately the same time. Staying in the warm womb of the shower stall became foolishness. She was drying her heat-flushed body when the doorbell rang, shattering the silence as well as her fragile state of mind. Gasping with surprise, she clung to the towel and stared toward the other room, unsure whether or not she should answer it. When she didn't respond to the summons, whoever was at the door gave up the buzzer and resorted to a fist. Probably the police after more answers.

"Chantal? Are you there?"

Dylan! The sound of his voice snapped the spell binding her. A relief she didn't even bother analyzing swept through her. Tossing the towel aside, she tugged a short terry robe over her damp body. Without bothering to wrap up her hair which was still dripping wet, she ran to the living room, her bare feet leaving damp marks on the plush silver carpet. Throwing back the dead bolt, she swung the door wide.

Dylan seemed to fill the opening. Dressed in jeans, cowboy boots and his bomber jacket, he looked intensely masculine, inordinately strong…unbelievably safe. Without a thought to the consequences, she launched herself at him, twining her arms around his neck, pressing her face against him and breathing in the heady scents of warm man and spicy cologne.

Placing his palms on either side of her head, Dylan took a step back and searched her face. If she expected concern, she was disappointed. Anger simmered in the depths of his dark eyes. "Are you all right?" he growled.

She nodded but felt the tears start again. "Don't be mad, Dylan," she choked out, laying her palm against his cheek. He stiffened and a look of surprise flickered across his face. "Please, just hold me."

Half lifting her, Dylan stepped through the door and kicked it shut with his foot. Then he drew her into his arms, cupped the back of her head with his big hand and crushed her to his chest. "It's going to be okay," he murmured.

For long moments they just stood there, silent, motionless, while Chantal drew strength from him and let his nearness absorb the last remnants of her fear. As the tension ebbed, she relaxed against him. She was about to tell him she was all right when she recognized a new tension building between them. His nearness no longer offered her the comfort she craved; instead, it was a source of stimulation. She became aware of the subtle shifting of his heartbeats from slow and steady to a faster, more erratic rhythm. His body, whose strength had promised security, now held the promise of excitement.

Pressed against him from knee to chin, she was acutely cognizant of the fact that she was naked beneath the short robe and that his thighs weren't the only portion of his anatomy that was rock-hard.

She'd done no more than acknowledge those facts when he took her face between his palms again. The only sound she could hear was the wild beating of her heart pounding in her ears—or was it their one heart beating together, the sound transmitted through his fingertips?

He tipped back her head and looked down at her with hot, hungry eyes. A reciprocal hunger gnawed at her. Without speaking, she knew he was offering her a chance to stop what was about to happen between them. Though her intellect whispered that nothing but heartache lay ahead, she couldn't say the words to halt the encroaching madness. It had been too long since she'd wanted a man the way she wanted Dylan Garvey.

Dylan worked his fingers through the wet hair of her temples, his fingertips outlining the shape of her ears while his thumbs traced the sweep of her dark, winged eyebrows, the straightness of her patrician nose and the exotic angle of her cheekbones. His touch grazed her temple, and she winced. His hands stilled. Frowning, he pushed back the wet fall of her hair. An angry-looking half circle marred the creamy flesh near her right eyebrow.

"What's this?"

She lifted her hand and fingered the raw place. "From the gun, I guess."

Dylan swore. "It's a burn. The barrel was hot after he made those warning shots, and the sonofa—"

Chantal put her fingers over his mouth, silencing the epithet. "It's okay."

Locking her face between the vice of his hands once more, he scrubbed his thumb over her parted lips. Chantal took the rough pad between her teeth in a gentle bite.

Dylan growled deep in his throat and grabbed double fistfuls of her wet hair. Chantal gave a small cry as he backed her roughly against the wall, pinning her there with the weight of his body. Rather than repel her, the violence triggered a reciprocal response in her. Danger and excitement meant being alive, and it was a state she wanted to revel in. She was alive, able to smell and taste and feel...and he smelled so good and felt so wonderful that she wanted to experience life and Dylan to the fullest.

Her lower body sagged against him, and a harsh breath hissed between his teeth. The look in his eyes was as exciting as it was dangerous, but Chantal stood her ground. She yanked his T-shirt from his jeans and slid her hands beneath it, letting her fingernails graze his hair-dusted stomach as she shifted her legs apart. The subtle movement enabled him to move deeper into the cleft of her thighs.

He untied the sash of her robe. She expected him to touch her, but instead, he feathered his hands along her collarbones and eased the terry covering off her shoulders and down her arms. Rivulets of water trickled from her hair, down her back and shoulders...between her breasts.

"Please," she whispered, needing him to touch her. Instead, he took a step back, holding her at arms' length and feasting his eyes on her. A small part of her wanted to hide from the blatant desire in his eyes, but mostly she wanted to take his hands in hers and make him touch her. As if he could read her mind, he laced his fingers through hers and, jerking her arms up over her wet head, pinned the backs of her hands against the wall.

Desire burned in his eyes. "Please what?"

"Kiss me."

He did. His mouth moved with savage hunger over her face, kissing her eyebrows, her closed eyes, her cheekbones, the corners of her mouth and her chin which he captured in a gentle love bite—everywhere but her lips.

He was playing with her, driving her crazy. She wanted to curse him and did. One of his rare smiles lifted the corners of his hard mouth. Leaning forward, he trailed his tongue from the valley between her breasts to the hollow of her throat and on up to the lobe of her ear, lapping up the trail of water that dripped from her hair.

The touch of his tongue against her sensitive flesh was like an electrical shock. She trembled beneath his touch. Nerve endings sizzled. The deepest part of her womanhood melted. Still, he hadn't touched her body with his hands. She would probably shatter into a million pieces if he did. The wanting was devastating now.

"Damn you!" she rasped, trying in vain to wriggle free. With her hands still imprisoned above her head, his open mouth crashed into hers, his tongue delving into the warm wetness of her mouth while, between her thighs, his slowly undulating hips ground against the throbbing mound of her femininity. A moan struggled up from her throat, and she strained to get closer, wanting, needing, to feel him deep inside her. Wanting, needing, for him to want her as much as she did him. She couldn't remember when she'd felt this all-consuming desire to take as well as to be taken. She yearned to touch him, to feel the smoothness of his flesh beneath her fingers.

Thought stopped when he released her and scooped her up into a close embrace. He carried her with ease through the apartment to the pale pink-and-white bedroom with its floral paintings and Battenberg lace. He placed her in the middle of the bed, took off his jacket and tore his T-shirt over his head. He sat down to take off his boots, but he wasn't fast enough. She scrambled off the edge of the bed and began to tug at one. His socks flew in two different directions. Together they peeled his jeans down long, muscled legs that boasted a sprinkling of dark hair. He stripped off his briefs and tossed them to the floor.

Later she would remember that his body was as perfect as she'd expected—muscles well-defined, perfectly proportioned. But her immediate thought was centered on putting out the fire he'd started inside her. He reached for her, and she used her weight to unbalance him. They fell together on the softness of the bed. Her breasts were crushed beneath his broad chest; the hardness of him pressed against the softness of her belly.

When he ducked his head and took the tip of her breast into his mouth, she cried out, tossed about by a maelstrom of sensation. Then he touched her. She gasped in pleasure while his fingers worked the age-old magic. She pressed closer, moving her hips in an effort to assuage the spiraling need.

Release came in a surge of feeling that undulated through her in wave after wave of pleasure, bringing a cry to her lips and a surge of love to her heart. His mouth caressing her breasts, he brought her to a second climax. She tried to hold on to him when he moved away, but he wouldn't be held. As she lay breathing heavily while the last aftershocks of desire rippled through her, she saw him pull a small package from his billfold.

Seconds later, he leaned over her. Their eyes locked. Without so much as a kiss, he nudged her thighs apart and entered her with a single shattering thrust. She gasped in surprise and pleasure—how could there be this much pleasure again?—and her nails dug into the flesh of his buttocks.

He whispered in her ear, something naughty, something that turned her on. She whispered a taunt back to him and a grim smile curved his mouth. He wasn't gentle; she didn't want him to be. She'd nearly forgotten how satisfying uninhibited sex could be. It had been so long....

Later—moments later? hours later?—Dylan relaxed against her, his weight a burden she bore gladly. His cheek rested against hers; her fingertips traced hieroglyphics on his sweat-dampened back. Her flesh glowed. Contentment curled inside her. Weariness washed over her. Sleep called. She felt utterly feminine. Supremely confident. Humble. Happy. She couldn't recall ever feeling so fully satisfied. She couldn't remember ever feeling so alive.

It was inevitable that Dylan got up, and when he had, he'd discovered that the condom had broken. There had been a moment's concern that his assurances soon soothed. She had thought little about it in the weeks that followed—not until she'd returned to Louisiana and discovered that she was carrying his child....

His child. His son. Gone. Chantal pressed her palms against her aching breasts and fought back the threatening tears. Tears wouldn't help. But maybe prayers would. She closed her eyes and asked God to keep her baby safe, to help the authorities find him. Emotion and exhaustion claimed her. She fell asleep with a prayer on her lips and despair in her heart.

Chapter Four

Though he wasn't thrilled, Dylan's superior grudgingly granted him a ten-day leave of absence. Dylan figured that if they hadn't located the baby by then, the chances were that they wouldn't any time soon...if they did at all. He managed to book a seat on a red-eye flight that would arrive in New Orleans at some indecently early hour the following morning, which gave him less than two hours to get his things together. If he managed to make it to the airport, he figured he could be at Thibodaux General by the time they brought around the breakfast trays.

The plane was minutes to taking off when he burst down the tunnel and handed over his boarding pass. He settled into the plane seat and heaved a sigh of relief as the jet taxied down the runway and lifted into the air.

On his way at last, Dylan closed his eyes and opened his mind to the full implications of the news Chantal had sprung on him. His initial anger still simmered inside him. He had a son, and, if some lunatic hadn't kidnapped him, he would never have learned of the baby's existence. Dylan's jaw tightened. If Chantal had told him sooner, he could have been there for the baby's birth, could have seen him, held him. Though he was angry at having been denied that pleasure, he knew that actually seeing and touching the baby would have made the feeling of emptiness inside him harder to bear than it already was. He wasn't sure he could forgive Chantal for robbing him of one of the things he most wanted, something his marriage to Carole had denied him.

Thinking of Carole brought a sigh. It had been a long time since he'd thought about his ex-wife, but considering Chantal's news, it seemed like a perfect time to take a good look at all his past mistakes and losses. Though he had celebrated the fourth anniversary of his divorce three months before with a bottle of cheap wine and a masochistic look through his photo albums, the failure of his marriage still ate at him. As painful as that failure was, Dylan knew he'd been to blame for the breakup of his marriage. Ready to settle down and mistaking passion for love, he'd married Carole Benning too quickly. He'd been so caught up in their physical relationship that he'd failed to see that they had basic differences in the way they viewed life.

Part of the problem was his occupation. The Garvey family had been turning out cops for three generations, and Dylan had never considered doing anything else. But, like so many other cops' wives, Carole couldn't take the pressures, the long lonely hours or the worry. She'd tried to adjust, but she was from a nine-to-five family, and Dylan's hours were erratic at best. Even though she knew he wanted a family, she'd balked at bringing a baby into the world. After all, when he left for work, she had no guarantee he would make it home at the end of his shift.

They might have overcome that hurdle if it hadn't been for the other, more serious problem: himself. Carole's most constant complaint was that he wasn't sensitive to her need for gentleness and understanding, but it wasn't until she finally filed for divorce that she told him she couldn't stand being married to a man who was so hard and insensitive, a man too hard and insensitive to make either a decent husband or father.

Dylan had been furious. Worse than that, he'd been crushed, though it had taken him weeks to admit it. It was months before he got far enough past the anger and pain to realize that her complaint might have some validity.

Carole had been wrong when she'd accused him of not being sensitive to her needs. He wasn't unaware of them, and he just didn't know how to deal with them. He had no idea what to do when she cried, especially when he didn't have a clue as to why she cried. Her woman's tears made him feel big and clumsy and inadequate. They reduced him to a pile of mush, and he wasn't able to say or do a thing. His usual reaction was to leave the house until she worked through the problem herself.

And, if there was a lack of gentleness in him, it was because he'd been born into a family that wasn't prone to demonstrations of affection. He'd grown up with a father who had taunted and whipped such inclinations out of him. Patrick Garvey had been a man's man, intolerant of anything that smacked of the gentler emotions in his son. His philosophy was that men provided the money, and women provided the tenderness—but only in measured doses for their sons. Dylan was praised when he got hurt and didn't cry, when he creamed another player in a football game, when he KO'd an opponent in college boxing.

Though he considered the ground his father walked on to be hallowed, his early words of love had been scoffed at, his every gesture of physical caring rebuffed. Hugs and kisses—what few there were of them—were doled out to Dylan's sisters. If Patrick ever said "I love you," it was to his wife, though Dylan never heard him say the words. If he were still alive, Patrick would no doubt be thrilled at how well his son had learned his lessons.

Dylan soon found that if he didn't make the overtures, he didn't have to deal with the rejection. He grew to manhood believing that he didn't need the tender things of life, but there were times—especially when his father died—that he'd needed desperately to reach out to someone. He'd passed by Patrick's coffin, his back rigid, his eyes dry. Patrick Garvey had died without ever telling Dylan he loved him, without ever knowing how much he was loved by his son.

It was no wonder he'd mistaken sex for love with Carole. For the first time in his life, he was touched and kissed and petted, and he loved it. He couldn't get enough, in fact. Learning that touching didn't—shouldn't—always lead to passion was a lesson he learned his first year of marriage, a hard, much-needed lesson.

For a while after the divorce, he'd hated Patrick Garvey for what he'd done to him, for all the things he'd denied him, for molding him into his own image. For a while after the demise of his marriage, Dylan was careful to get involved only with women who weren't looking for a serious relationship, not that there were that many of them. He'd soon learned that even a relationship based on sex demanded that he give a portion of himself, a portion he didn't know how to give, even if he'd been so inclined. The truth was, he was no closer now to being the kind of man Carole claimed every woman wanted than he'd ever been.

When he met Chantal, there hadn't been anyone for a long time, and he'd convinced himself their meeting was meant to be. If she'd been managing the casino at any other time, if there hadn't been that rash of jewelry thefts while she was there, if he hadn't been assigned to that particular case, they never would have met.

The first time he'd seen her, he'd been drawn to her exotic looks. Tall, willowy, but with high, full breasts, she was exactly the type to catch his eye. It didn't hurt that she had thick, shoulder-length chestnut hair that flowed down her back like a swath of russet-hued silk, almond-shaped hazel eyes and those full, model's lips that begged to be kissed. As she mingled with the casino's customers, she was polite and friendly, but there was a cool reserve about her that intrigued him. Kissing those lips became his goal. Making love with her became his favorite fantasy. When it finally happened, it had been everything he'd dreamed it would be. More.

It was as if divine providence had made her for his embrace. Her curves and angles fit his like a key in a lock. She was soft and warm and giving. As hungry as he was, she had devoured him with her need, had whetted his own until it threatened to consume them both. He wasn't sure if he'd ever felt such an overwhelming rush of emotion as he climaxed. As crazy as it sounded, it was more than a physical release. It seemed that, like the poems and songs often claimed, they had melded body and soul. Even crazier, for the first time in his adult life, he felt as if he'd come home.

They'd made love all night and fallen asleep in each other's arms. He'd forgotten how nice that could be. When he woke up, she was gone, and panic gripped him. But she was only in the kitchen making breakfast. He stayed the day, and, after lunch, they'd whiled away the afternoon playing strip poker and making love. He'd hated to go home, hated leaving her, which wasn't like him.

He told himself it was because he'd met his match sexually. Though he knew she wasn't the kind to play fast and loose, she was no shrinking violet when it came to taking what she wanted from a man, and that was quite a turn on. If the time he'd spent with her was any indication, their lovemaking had only fanned the flames of a desire he suspected it would take a lifetime to burn out, a suspicion that gave him pause. What, exactly, did that indicate? That he wanted more than an affair? That even with his bad batting average he was thinking of something more permanent?

Maybe. He wasn't sure what that something was, but he was reasonably sure he wanted it.

He told himself his thoughts were insane, that he hardly knew her, that it was lunacy to look beyond the next time they were together. Hadn't life taught him not to count on anything or anyone but himself? Not to dream beyond tomorrow? Afraid to delve too deeply into the feelings churning inside him, relying on time to help work things out, all he could do was worship her with his body and hope it was enough.

As it turned out, it wasn't. The next time he'd seen her, Chantal had made it very clear that she wanted no part of him or any tomorrows he might be dreaming of....

Dylan hadn't seen or talked to Chantal in two days. First he got tied up with a new case that required his being out of town briefly, and when he did get a chance to call, she seemed distant, reserved.

Worried, he'd gone to her apartment as soon as he could. As she had the night she'd been taken captive, she came to the door in her robe. This time she didn't throw herself into his embrace. Arms crossed over her breasts, she stood and looked at him as if he were a stranger. Something was very wrong. And as usual, he didn't know what to do about it.

"Second thoughts?" he asked, stepping inside and closing the door.

"And third and fourth," she blurted. "How about you?"

He was solemn as he shook his dark head. "No. None."

She shrugged and attempted a smile. "I guess I don't take making love with a stranger lightly."

She turned and started to walk away, but he grabbed her arm and forced her to look at him. "Why are you acting like this? And why are you giving me the brush-off?"

"It isn't a brush-off," she denied, turning her face away. "I just needed some space."

"Yeah? Well, it sure as hell feels like one." He took her chin between his thumb and fingers and forced her to face him. "Look at me when I'm talking to you."

She knocked his hand away. "Okay," she said, her voice as sharp as an ice pick. "I'm looking at you. Are you happy?" When he didn't answer, she closed her eyes for a moment. When she opened them he saw cool determination there. "It happened too fast, Dylan. It should never have happened at all. We're too different for anything to ever work between us."

"It worked pretty well the other night," he reminded her, stung by her assessment of their future together.

She shook her head. "Don't you see?" she cried. "That was just good sex—"

"Well, thanks for that much, anyway." Sarcasm dripped from his voice.

She took a deep breath and shoved her hands in the pockets of her robe. He could almost see her reining in her anger. His escalated.

"I'm sorry if you're upset," she said. "I'm willing to take full responsibility for my actions, but I was scared . . . and damn glad to be alive."

Dylan released her and, holding his palms up, began to back away. "Spare me your rationalizations.

You want to forget it happened? Or better yet, pretend it didn't? You got it! It's pretty obvious you aren't interested in a repeat performance." He turned toward the door.

"Dylan!"

He turned. There was a censure in her eyes he didn't understand. And resignation.

"There's something else."

"I thought so."

"You lied to me."

He frowned. "I don't know what the hell you're talking about."

"Why didn't you tell me you were a policeman?"

For long moments, he could only stare at her. He shook his head slowly. "Is that what this is all about? You're mad at me because I didn't tell you I was a cop?"

"I'm mad because you *lied* to me," she said, grating the word between clenched teeth.

He took a step toward her, stopped and placed his hands on his hips. "I didn't lie. I was working on a case, damn it! There's a difference."

"You could have told me."

"When I'm working, I can't tell anyone." He paced the small room and came back to stand in front of her. "Look, when you work vice, lives depend on how believable your cover is. I'm not talking about just my life, but the lives of the people I work with."

"Spare me your rationalizations," she said, flinging his earlier words back at him. "I've had too many other men lie to me in the past. I'm not anxious to get involved with another one."

"I'm not other men, and in case you haven't noticed, baby, you're already involved."

"Having sex with a man doesn't mean there are any strings attached. I don't need you or any other man to make me happy."

It hurt. Dylan told himself it shouldn't, but it did. Still, he'd be damned if he let her know it. "Except to scratch your particular itch from time to time, right?" he taunted.

The color drained from her face. "You make me sound—" She broke off. "I was overwrought. Scared."

"So you keep saying. I could buy that the first time we made love. But what about the third and fourth?" he taunted. "At least when I want a woman I'm truthful enough to admit it without looking for excuses to justify my actions."

"Don't pretend that my breaking this off is some sort of big deal that's going to affect your future happiness," she told him, launching the best attack she could under the circumstances.

"Don't tell me how to feel!" he snapped. A muscle in his jaw knotted, and he pointed an accusatory finger at her. "You play dirty, lady."

She raised her rounded chin and met his hard gaze with a defiant one. "That's just it. I'm not playing."

Neither was he. Dylan had never been more serious in his life. He thought of his daydreams, of his tentative feeling that this thing with Chantal might lead to something else, something permanent. With his heart beating painfully, he had cocked his head to one side and regarded her with a cold look. "Yeah, well, you should lay it on the line with your next victim...it might save a lot of hard feelings...."

The "fasten seat belts" bell pinged, rousing Dylan from his memories. Even after nine months it hurt to remember. Obviously Chantal had been hurt by someone in the past, but damn it, so had anyone who'd ever imagined they were in love. Getting hurt didn't mean locking yourself away and refusing to get involved again. It made a person more careful, and if he was lucky, he learned from his mistakes. Dylan's mouth twisted in a wry smile. Which is what Chantal would claim she'd done. She'd learned not to give in to her feelings, not to surrender her heart to anyone who might cause her any pain.

Having suffered through his share of misery, Dylan understood her thinking. What he didn't understand was how she could just set her mind against it and keep the feelings from happening. It must be a nifty trick if you could master it.

He sighed and exited the plane, then headed toward the car rental agency next to the airport. He was looking forward to his reunion with Chantal with all the enthusiasm of Daniel entering the lion's den. Still, a part of him couldn't wait to see her again. Whatever it was he felt for her, he knew he was heading into heartache and needed all the defenses he could muster, but the best he could manage was a quick spruce-up at a gas station near the rental agency.

In the tiny, antiseptic-smelling cubicle, he brushed his teeth, splashed some water on his face and combed his hair. He needed to shave; his deep purple short-sleeve shirt was wrinkled, and he needed a good cup of coffee before he went on to the hospital. He hadn't been able to sleep at all during the flight, and he was exhausted. His eyes were red-rimmed and felt as if someone had thrown a handful of sand in them. As he tossed a fistful of paper toweling into the trash can, he regarded his rugged visage in the wavy mirror and decided he'd have to do.

Suddenly, he stopped. Who was he trying to kid? He was concerned about his appearance because he wanted to look his best for Chantal. The realization brought a scowl to his face. Furious with himself, he stormed out of the gas station, got into the rental car and slammed the door. He couldn't wait to get this over with.

As he predicted, he entered the hospital just as they were bringing the breakfast trays around. He found Chantal's room number and was standing outside her door gathering himself when an aide started in with her breakfast.

The woman smiled at him as she passed. "Is it okay if I take it to her?" he asked.

"Sure. Are you family?"

"No."

"Oh. Isn't it just terrible about the baby being taken and all?" the woman said, relinquishing the tray.

Dylan's heart plummeted. "Yeah. Terrible."

The woman gave him a coy smile. "If you aren't family, you must be a friend."

Dylan could tell she wouldn't be satisfied until her curiosity was appeased. "Not exactly," he told her. "I'm the baby's father."

The smile on the aide's face faded. "Oh, I'm so sorry. I'm sure you don't want to talk about it."

"On the contrary, Ms.—" he glanced at her name tag "—Robbins, I'm with the Atlantic City Police Department, and if the local authorities okay it, I'll be doing a great deal of talking about it."

Her eyes grew wide. "Oh. Well..."

Dylan gave her one of his rare, but devastating smiles. The news would be all over the hospital in no time. "I'll be seein' you." He shouldered the door open and prepared to confront his past.

He was granted a slight reprieve.

Chantal was asleep, her hand curled beneath her cheek. Instead of the hospital garb he expected, she was wearing a bright teal satin and ecru lace gown that dipped over her breasts, which looked fuller than he remembered. His heart skipped a beat, and he gave a silent curse. Her face was fuller, too. She'd gained some weight, but that was natural for pregnant women, he supposed. Her hair was longer. From where he stood, he wasn't sure if the shadowy smudges beneath her eyes were caused from exhaustion or her dark lashes. She made a sound, something between a shudder and a sob, that tugged at his heart.

Dylan set down the tray on a nearby table and approached the bed. He eased into the chair beside her and let his eyes roam over her face at will, concluding that the shadows under her eyes were the result of weariness. Her lips were dry and cracked. She looked so drained, so vulnerable, lying there in the white hospital bed.

But looks could be deceiving. He'd learned the hard way that Chantal Robichaux was far from helpless and vulnerable. Remembering the soft pliancy of her mouth as it hungrily devoured his was counterpro-

ductive under the circumstances. Worse than counterproductive. It was downright masochistic.

He pushed the memory away and forced himself to
remember that this was the woman who had kept the
knowledge of his child from him. Still, it was hard to
separate the anger from the haunting memories of
their shared need.

As if she could feel the intensity of his gaze boring
into her, Chantal stirred and opened her light brown
eyes. For a moment, she looked sleepy, almost dazed,
and then, when she realized he was sitting next to her,
the look in her eyes grew wary.

"Dylan," she said on a breathless whisper.

"Good morning," he said, his voice just barely
pitched at civility.

Pushing the hair from her face in a typically feminine gesture of embarrassment, she tried to sit up
straighter. A grimace pulled at her lips. Dylan frowned
at the small sign of discomfort. "Wh-when did you get
in?"

"Just a few minutes ago." He nodded his head toward the tray. "I brought your breakfast in."

"I'm not hungry." She reached for the controls and
began to raise the head of the bed, careful to keep her
gaze averted.

"How about something to drink, then?"

"Juice sounds good, thanks."

Dylan suspected that she was holding on to her
control with great difficulty. So was he. He put on his
coolest, most professional demeanor. It would never
do for him to let her know how upset he was over the
baby's disappearance or over seeing her again. He was
seething with questions. He wanted to know his son's

name, how much he weighed, who he looked like...but he sensed that now wasn't the time. Instead, he went to the tray and opened a container of orange juice. Glass in hand, he turned and started back toward the bed, taking a swallow as he went. If she was surprised by his actions, she didn't show it. After all, they'd shared much more than a glass of juice.

"Have you heard anything?" he asked, handing her the drink.

Their fingers brushed as she took it from him. Her hand trembled, and she wrapped the fingers of her other hand around the glass to steady it. "No. Cade says they'll probably ask me to help them with a composite drawing today."

"Probably. If you're up to it."

"I have to be," she said, her voice quivering. She raised the juice to her lips and took a sip.

"Chantal." Her gaze jerked to his. "Why didn't you tell me before now?"

"I told you—"

"I know what you told me," he interrupted. "But I want to know the real reason."

"I was afraid to."

"Afraid to? Why?"

"For a lot of reasons that made sense at the time. I was afraid you'd think I was lying about the baby being yours. Afraid you'd try to take him away from me. Strangely enough, even though it makes no sense, I was even afraid you wouldn't care."

"Why would you think I wouldn't care?"

"You don't seem like the...fatherly type."

It hurt. Like Carole, Chantal didn't seem to think he would make a good father. But damn it! He should have been offered the opportunity to try. He wanted to lash out at her, but knew she was in no condition to hold up her end of the quarrel.

"Don't you think that's being a bit judgmental? You don't particularly seem like the motherly type."

She looked surprised by the question and his observation. "I...maybe you're right, but I didn't know how you'd feel about having a child with me. After all, what we had was little more than a one-night stand."

Chapter Five

Little more than a one-night stand? The silence in the room grew deafening. Pain. Disappointment. Anger. Dylan was experiencing them all in varying degrees. How could she possibly consider what they'd shared a one-night stand? Of course, he reminded himself, she had no way of knowing his feelings; he'd gone to great lengths not to commit himself with words, but surely she could tell from the way he kissed her...from the way he'd loved her far into the night... that it was more than a casual sexual encounter.

He was trying to think of something nonconfrontational to say when there was a soft knock on the door. He looked up and saw a pretty dark-haired woman and a tall man bearing the Robichaux good looks standing there. Dylan rose.

"Hey, sis," the man said, ushering his wife into the room. His greeting was directed at Chantal, but his unwavering gaze was focused on Dylan.

"Hi," Chantal said, attempting a smile. Her uneasy gaze volleyed between her brother and Dylan. She brushed back a lock of hair. "Dylan, this is my brother, Cade, and his wife, Shiloh. Cade, Shiloh, this is Dylan Garvey."

Though she didn't say the words, "the baby's father" might just as well have been tacked on to the introduction.

The two men sized each other up as Dylan rounded the foot of the bed. Though he knew Cade Robichaux wrote computer games for a living, the older man didn't look as if his work had made him go soft. As a matter of fact, he didn't look like the type Dylan would want to tangle with at all. Unsmiling, he offered his hand to each of the Robichauxs in turn. Shiloh's hand was soft and small, but her handshake was as firm and no-nonsense as her husband's.

"It's good to finally get to meet you," Chantal's brother said.

Dylan searched both the comment and Cade's face for signs of sarcasm but detected nothing but a reserved politeness in either.

"I'm sorry it has to be under such conditions," Cade added.

"So am I," Dylan said, unaware that his eyes darkened with pain at the oblique reminder of why he was there.

The social amenities satisfied, Cade and his wife turned their attention to Chantal. Shiloh went to the bed and pressed her cheek to Chantal's. "How are you, honey?"

"I'm okay," Chantal said, but her eyes filled with tears.

"I'm so sorry about all this," Shiloh said, emotion evident in her own voice. "What can we do?"

"Nothing." There was no hope in the reply. Then she added, "Just pray."

"We are."

Dylan felt a giant fist squeeze his heart. Prayer wasn't an avenue of help he'd chosen often in his adult life. He'd gotten too used to relying on himself. At the moment, seeking help from a greater power held tremendous appeal. He wasn't aware that his face held a look of bleak despair. He was wondering how things had gotten so tangled up when he heard Shiloh say his name.

"I beg your pardon," he said, forcing his thoughts back to the present. "I was thinking."

Her friendly smile made the bridge of her tip-tilted nose crinkle and went a long way toward putting him at ease. "Thinking? More like sleeping on your feet," she teased. "I asked what time you got in."

"Just a few minutes ago."

She waved a tiny hand. "Well, no wonder you're a little out of things. You must be exhausted if you've been up all night." There was genuine concern both in her eyes and her voice with its soft Tennessee drawl.

One corner of his mouth hiked up in a weary half smile. "I am pretty beat."

"Cade and I would like you to stay with us at Magnolia Manor while you're here, wouldn't we?" she said, turning and dimpling up at her husband.

Dylan's surprised gaze moved to Cade, who looked only marginally nonplussed. Chantal looked horrified.

"That's sweet of you, Shiloh," she said, "but I'm sure Dylan—"

"Would be foolish to refuse," Cade interrupted. "How often does a person get a chance to stay in a one-hundred-fifty-year-old plantation house?" He smiled at Dylan. "Besides, Shiloh is a genuine, certified chef, and her cooking is to die for. There are people in town who've been waiting two years for an invitation to dinner."

Dylan didn't think staying with Chantal's family would be a very comfortable situation, but with them both insisting, it seemed churlish to refuse. He shot a quick glance at Chantal. She didn't look pleased by the offer, either. "Thanks," he said, albeit reluctantly. "I appreciate the invitation."

Cade smiled and nodded. "I'll draw you a map."

"Great." Dylan hoped he sounded more enthusiastic than he felt. He had the feeling that under different circumstances, he and Cade Robichaux might have become friends. As things stood, he figured he could look forward to the third degree when he got to the plantation.

"You feel free to drive on out whenever you're ready," Shiloh offered. "We'll be there."

"Thank you, I will."

That settled to her obvious satisfaction, Shiloh turned her attention back to Chantal. "Now then, how about you? Did you sleep?"

"When they finally came in about midnight with a sleeping pill," Chantal said.

Shiloh patted her sister-in-law's hand. "That's understandable. Are you in a lot of pain?"

Dylan didn't miss the dismayed glance Chantal flicked toward him. Pain? Why would she be in pain? He'd always supposed that once the baby was born, the hurting would be over. Was there something wrong with Chantal he didn't know about?

"It's more like acute discomfort than actual pain," she said.

"You never were one to complain," Cade, who was busy drawing the map, said with a shake of his head.

Shiloh sauntered to the breakfast tray. "What did you have for breakfast?" She peeked beneath the stainless-steel covers. "Obviously nothing."

"I don't have much of an appetite," Chantal said in defense. "It's probably the medication."

Shiloh gave Chantal a stern look. "You've got to eat if you want to get your strength back."

"I know."

"I'll keep after her," Dylan said.

"Good." Shiloh smiled at him. Going to Cade, she looped her arm through his. "Well, darlin', now that we know she's in good hands, I guess we can go on back home."

"I'm ready if you are." Cade handed the map to Dylan.

Dylan folded the small piece of notepaper in half and tucked it into his shirt pocket. "I'll walk out with you. I need to find a vending machine so I can get a cup of coffee." What he really wanted to do was ask about Chantal.

"Sure."

"I'll be back in a minute," Dylan said to Chantal.

The Robichauxs said their goodbyes and Dylan followed them into the hallway.

"The house is easy to find," Shiloh said. "If you get lost, just ask anyone for directions."

"I will." Dylan scrubbed a hand down his whisker-stubbled cheek. His weary gaze found Cade's. "I appreciate your kindness." He shrugged. "Under the circumstances, it's unexpected. I don't know what she's told you, but I want you to know that if I'd known about the baby sooner, I'd have been here."

"Actually, she hasn't told us much at all. I tried to get her to call, but she wouldn't. I don't know what happened between you and my sister, and I don't know what your feelings are toward her. I do know she's as stubborn as a Missouri mule and that she's carrying a lot of baggage around from her first marriage."

"Aren't we all?" Dylan replied.

"Chantal's an adult, and she knows the score. I'm certainly not going to judge you. Whatever happened between the two of you, happened. Right now, our main concern is to get the baby back. Maybe the rest will sort itself out."

"I hope so." Cade's attitude made Dylan feel much better. Chantal's brother was one of those increasingly rare species, a decent, fair man. "Have the police got any clues?"

"Nothing beyond a description Chantal gave them. They want her to help put together a composite drawing some time today."

Dylan nodded. "Who's in charge of the investigation?"

"Phil Rousseau. He's a good man."

"I think I'll go by and have a talk with him a little later . . . see if there's anything I can do."

"I thought you might want to be involved," Cade said with a smile and a nod. "After all, it's your child, too."

"My only child." Dylan said, unaware of the wistfulness in his voice.

Cade and Shiloh exchanged a quick glance that he intercepted. Damn it! He didn't want their pity. He straightened his weary shoulders and directed his next question to Shiloh. "I heard you asking Chantal about being in pain. Is something wrong?"

"Chantal went through a long, hard labor." She gave him a wry smile. "In the end, your son was so big they had to do a cesarean section. She'll be a little sore for a few days."

"How much did he weigh?" he queried, wanting to find out as much about the baby as possible.

"Nine pounds, one ounce," Shiloh said.

"Nine pounds. And that's pretty big?" he asked.

"Let's just say he was half grown when he got here," Shiloh said dryly, but her eyes twinkled with that teasing light Dylan was becoming familiar with.

"Who does he look like?"

"Like himself. He has blue eyes—most babies do at first—and a headful of dark hair. He has plump little cheeks, and, as Chantal said, I think he has your mouth." She smiled at him. "He's a beautiful baby, Dylan, but why wouldn't he be? He has beautiful parents."

A feeling of acute sorrow swept through Dylan. Up until the last few minutes, he had been reacting to the baby as something—an item—he'd missed out on, been lied to about. While there was no doubt that he was suffering, his pain had been driven by anger at what Chantal had denied him. Talking to Shiloh about the baby made him seem more real, somehow. Hearing her describe him, knowing Chantal saw a part of him in their child, Dylan became aware of a pain rooted in a deep feeling of loss. He swallowed hard. "Thanks."

"We'll find him," Cade said, squeezing Dylan's shoulder in a gesture designed to comfort.

Dylan looked up at Chantal's brother. "I'm sure as hell going to give it my best shot."

Shiloh and Cade were barely our of earshot when she hooked her arm through his, leaned against him and murmured, "So what do you think?"

Cade looked thoughtful. "What do I think? Hmm. I don't know why, but I think I like him."

"Me, too," she said with a smile. "That's why I asked him to stay with us."

Cade slid his arm around her shoulders and laughed. "And I thought you asked him to stay with us so you could pump him about how he feels about Chantal."

"Cade Robichaux! You know I'd never do that." Shiloh grinned up at him. "I asked him so *you* could pump him about how he feels about Chantal."

Cade pushed open the glass door that led to the parking lot and ushered her through. "Don't worry your pretty head, *chère,* I have every intention of doing that."

"I thought so." Her forehead knitted in thought as she skipped along beside him, trying to keep up with his ground-eating stride. "He's very handsome. It's easy to see why Chantal would fall for him. Most women are drawn to men with that aura of danger about them."

"That's interesting," Cade observed. "So why did you fall for me? I'm about as dangerous as the threat of sunstroke on a cloudy day."

"I'm not most women," Shiloh said. "Besides, your dangerous side is there, it's just less visible. You're the still-waters-run-deep type. You can just be pushed so far and then—watch out!"

"I have a feeling that Dylan's temper has a quick trigger."

"No doubt," Shiloh agreed. "But he has a sensitive side, too. Did you see his face when you said you wished you could have met him under better circumstances?"

"Yeah, I did. And when Chantal told you there was nothing to do but pray, I don't think I've ever seen such a look of despair on a person's face. This has gotten to him."

"Well, you'd have to be a pretty tough character not to feel something at losing a child," Shiloh said, thinking briefly of the baby she'd lost and how it had almost cost her her sanity and her marriage. "I suspect that beneath that rough exterior, Dylan Garvey has a heart that can be touched, otherwise, Chantal would never have fallen for him. I also have a sneaking suspicion that he's a guy who could use a whole lot of love in his life."

While Dylan was out in the corridor with Shiloh and Cade, Chantal was trying to calm her nerves and her fears. When she'd opened her eyes and seen Dylan sitting next to the bed, she'd been surprised that he'd arrived so soon and a little frightened of the calculating look in his eyes. Still, she couldn't deny that her heart had begun to race—and not in fear. The attraction she'd felt for him in New Jersey was alive and well. She was less than thrilled to realize that he could affect her so strongly when she was so determined not to let him. But then, something about him had undermined her determination from the first, and now they had a child together.

She drew a shaky breath. Seeing Dylan again brought the past ten months into sharp focus. Even knowing hindsight was twenty-twenty, she realized she'd been a fool. While it was true that they had little in common and there wasn't much hope for them to have a future together, she'd behaved terribly in the way she'd gone about breaking things off.

Now she could see how she'd over-reacted to the news that he was a cop. She knew she had been quick to blame him for something he had no control over because she was afraid. Afraid of what he made her feel, afraid he didn't feel the same. So she'd made a big deal out of his "lie."

But as he'd pointed out the night before, she was the one who'd lied. Not only had she lied by omission by not telling him about the baby, she'd lied to herself about her feelings for him. She cared for him. She didn't know if it was love, or if it could lead to love, but whatever it was, she had refused to acknowledge it as anything more than great sex, a couple of good days with no future. She'd figured it would be easier on her own emotions if she laid out the rules, if she did the rejecting. But she'd figured wrong. The last months had been a lonely, frightening hell of her own making.

Anticipating the baby's birth had been the only bright spot on her horizon. The child would be a part of Dylan, a reminder of a time she never wanted to forget. And now that link to her past was gone.

Chantal fought the urge to scream out her misery and sorrow. She couldn't give in to the fears tearing her apart. They would give her another shot, but she didn't want to sleep. She wanted to be awake when they found her baby so that she could hold him close and breathe in that clean baby scent....

She heard a noise at the door, and Dylan came into the room, carrying his coffee. Alone again with their bittersweet memories and bitter accusations building between them, they regarded each other like two prize fighters sizing each other up before a championship bout. Chantal's heart began to beat heavily in her chest. She'd forgotten how big he was, how handsome. Forgotten how his slightly curly hair refused to be tamed and fell over his forehead in a rakish way that somehow underscored his masculinity instead of softening his hard good looks.

A twinge of embarrassment at how she must look to him made her glance away. She probably looked as if she'd been run through a wringer, as her momma used to say.

Dylan held his cup aloft. "Can I get you some?"

"No, thanks."

He leaned his broad shoulders against the far wall and crossed his right foot over the left, the toe of his tasseled loafer resting against the shining tile of the floor. "If you'll be okay by yourself for a while, I think I'll go to the police station and see if they've turned up anything new."

"I've been staying by myself," she said with a lift of her chin. "I'll be fine."

He nodded. "Can I pick up anything for you while I'm out? Cosmetics? Something to read?"

Did he think she needed cosmetics? she wondered, tucking her hair back behind her ear in a gesture that betrayed her mortification. Why was she upset about how he thought she looked, for goodness' sake? She should be furious at him for talking to her the way he had on the phone and before Cade and Shiloh had arrived. What was the matter with her, anyway? The emotions she'd always held in complete control were going up and down like a seesaw.

She gave a short, sharp laugh. "I don't think cosmetics are going to help much until I can do something with this hair. It wouldn't take any curl while I was pregnant."

He scowled. "I didn't mean—"

"It's okay," she interrupted, crossing her arms over her breasts in a defensive gesture.

Dylan used the opportunity to take a swallow of the strong-looking coffee, which he almost spewed across the room. "What the hell's in this stuff, anyway?" he sputtered.

For a moment, Chantal's heartache was forgotten. For a moment, she forgot all the bad things that had passed between them, all the trouble that was still to come. She couldn't help the smile that urged the corners of her lips upward. "Chicory," she said. "It's an acquired taste."

"Not in this lifetime," Dylan assured her.

This time her mouth curved fully. This time, it was Dylan who couldn't stop the abashed half smile from taking his lips. Simultaneously, they recalled other, happier times. Simultaneously, they remembered that now wasn't one of them. Their smiles died guilty, instant deaths, as if someone somewhere had flipped an imaginary switch.

Dylan pushed himself away from the wall and set down the cup. "I'd better be going." Chantal saw no need to answer. When he reached the door, he asked, "Can I bring you something for lunch?"

"I don't need anything," she said with a shake of her head.

It wasn't until he was gone that she realized that what she'd said could be easily misconstrued. And if it could be taken the wrong way, there was little doubt that that's exactly the way Dylan would take it.

Dylan held his hand out to the balding detective in charge of Thibodaux's Criminal Investigation Division. "Dylan Garvey, Atlantic City Police Department."

"Phil Rousseau." The detective's grip was firm, his smile was pleasant, but on the weary side. "You're a long way from home, aren't you?"

"Slightly," Dylan said.

Rousseau settled himself in the worn leather chair behind his scarred desk. He flipped open a small box, took out a cigar and bit off the end, which he spit into a concealed trash can. "What can I do for you, Mr. Garvey?" he asked, cocking the chair back and flipping back the top of an ancient silver lighter with a monogrammed *R.*

"You can tell me how the investigation is coming along on the baby that was taken from the hospital yesterday morning."

Rousseau puffed on the cigar a few times to make certain it was burning and blew a stream of smelly smoke upward. Leaning both forearms on the desk, he pinned Dylan with a jaundiced eye. "Why do you want to know?"

Dylan didn't blink beneath the detective's challenging stare. "I'm the baby's father."

"And you came down here from the big city to make sure us country bumpkins were doing our job, is that it?"

Dylan refused to rise to Rousseau's baiting. He didn't think the older man was an obnoxious cop; he suspected he'd inadvertently ruffled the guy's feathers. "I came down here because my baby is missing. I haven't even seen him yet, Detective Rousseau."

The calm statement went a long way toward softening Rousseau's attitude. He settled back in his chair. "I'm sorry. I was out of line."

Dylan shrugged. "No cop likes for another one to come in and try to take over his investigation, and that certainly isn't my intention. I would like to know what you have so far, what leads you're following, that sort of thing."

"That's fair enough," Rousseau said with a nod. "I'd like to ask you a couple of questions, too, if I may."

"Sure." Dylan sat back in his chair and laced his fingers together over his flat stomach.

"You and the baby's mother aren't married— right?"

"That's correct," Dylan said, his own feathers feeling a tad ruffled.

"Any particular reason why?"

"Any particular reason you need to know?" Dylan countered with a narrowing of his dark eyes. "I mean, is that information pertinent to the case?"

Instead of looking embarrassed, Rousseau met Dylan's insolent gaze head-on. "Actually, it is. If the breakup between the two of you was particularly unpleasant, and if you're a spiteful sort of guy, you could have had the baby taken yourself just to get back at the mother."

The disbelief in Dylan's eyes was unmistakable. "In case it's escaped your notice, I'm one of the good guys here."

"Wearing a badge doesn't always equate with being a good guy, Garvey, as you well know."

"Touché," Dylan said. One of his rare smiles made a brief appearance. "Actually, I'm pretty damned impressed over your speculation. The only thing wrong with it is that I didn't even know there was going to be a baby."

"The hell you say!"

"Hey, ask her," Dylan said with a lift of his massive shoulders. "I didn't find out about the baby until Chantal called me late last night and told me he'd been taken from the hospital. As you suggested, our parting wasn't the best."

"I see."

"Look, Detective Rousseau, I'm willing to cut out all this macho garbage if you are. All I want to do is find my baby."

Rousseau nodded. "We are working on it. Detective Adams from Missing Persons is in charge. I'm sending the artist over this afternoon and see if we can get a composite of the perpetrator." Seeing the question in Dylan's eyes, he added, "We would have done it yesterday, but Ms. Robichaux was so hysterical it would have been counterproductive."

Dylan felt as if the Thibodaux policeman had just kicked him in the gut. Hysterical? She'd seemed calm enough this morning. He scoured his mind for evidence of hysterical behavior on the phone the night before. Of course, she'd sounded upset, but then, he'd come down on her pretty hard.

"Once we get the drawing, we'll circulate it at the hospital and see if we can find anyone who saw her. Then we'll run it in the paper. In the meantime, we're checking all the general practitioners and pediatricians in the parish to see if she got any medical help for the baby."

"Have you checked the hospital records to see how many women have had miscarriages or lost a newborn in the past year?" Dylan asked.

"No, why?"

"Sometimes a woman who's lost a baby or knows she can't have one goes over the edge and decides to snatch someone else's. Didn't you see that movie on television a while back? The one where the woman took the month-old baby and tried to pass it off as a newborn."

Rousseau shook his head. "It was based on a true story," Dylan informed him. "It isn't the normal reaction by any means, but it can happen. It has happened."

"Makes sense. I'll get someone on it as soon as I can, but you may as well know we're swamped. We're a small department, and the last couple of weeks have been murder—" he grimaced at the unintentional pun "—literally. We had a heat-of-passion killing, a hit and run, a rape and a rash of burglaries, and we're shorthanded because of summer vacations."

Dylan whistled. "That's a lot of action for a town this size."

"Tell me. It's a combination of the heat and the economy. To top it all off, it'll be a full moon in a couple of nights."

Dylan understood too well. When there was a money shortage tempers got short, too. There were more burglaries, more cases of domestic violence. And full moons always seemed to bring out the worst in people. "I'd be glad to check on it myself," Dylan offered.

"I'm sorry, son, but you're way out of your jurisdiction. Besides, the chief would kick my butt all the way to Baton Rouge and back if I let someone else do the department's job."

Dylan wasn't happy, but he nodded his understanding. "Just keep me posted, will you?" he said, rising to his feet. "And I want to be there when the artist goes to the hospital."

"He'll be there about one."

"Then so will I." Dylan held out his hand. "It's been a pleasure, Detective Rousseau."

"Real interesting," Rousseau agreed.

Dylan left the police headquarters and headed back to the hospital via a discount store, where he bought Chantal a couple of magazines, a box of chocolates and a couple of paperback bestsellers. A wrong turn took him past a day care situated in a house whose pastel colors made it look like a confectioner's dream. He pulled the car to the curb, inexplicably drawn to the children playing in the fenced yard. He pressed a button and the window on the passenger side slid down, giving him uncensored access to the children and their games.

Two little girls caught his attention first. One was blond and smiling with dancing eyes that had to be blue. But the one who really called to him was dark-haired, dark-eyed and serious. She was trying to climb into a swing. As he watched her refuse help from the adult in charge, he could see the same emerging independence he imagined Chantal had exhibited as a child.

What happened, he wondered, to make such a difference in people and how they reacted to their world? Was it something inherited or learned? He suspected it was a little of both. He recalled Cade's comment about Chantal carrying a lot of baggage around from her marriage and wondered what her ex-husband had done to hurt her so badly. What kind of lies had he told that made truthfulness of dogmatic importance to her?

And why does it matter so much to you, after the way she lied about the baby? he thought, gripping the steering wheel tighter. He didn't know. Even though his mind was filled with questions that demanded answers, he was too exhausted to think; his brain was on overload. He knew that what he needed was several hours' sleep, but he wanted to be at the hospital when the police artist showed up. He glanced at his watch. By the time he stopped and had some lunch, it would be time to get back.

He was about to put the car in gear when a woman stepped onto the back porch of the soft aqua-and-pink house. "Tad! Your dad is here!"

As Dylan watched, a man exited the house and moved across the porch to the yard, which was toasted brown in the heat. A little boy—no more than four—abandoned the sandpile and flew toward his dad as fast as his sturdy legs would carry him.

Damn, the kid was cute. Dark hair cut short on top and longer in back. Tan skin that glowed with health. Dylan wasn't aware that a smile had taken claim of his mouth. It broadened as the man stooped and took the full impact of his son's body. With a loud whoop of laughter the man tumbled onto his back and lifted the child high above his head. High-pitched giggles and squeals of, "Again, Daddy, again!" floated through the climbing heat of the morning.

"No more, son. You're killing me." The man got to his feet, swung the boy up into his arms and held him close—forehead to forehead, nose to nose. From where he sat, Dylan couldn't hear the words, but he knew from their smiles and the looks on both faces that the man was telling the boy that he loved him.

They disappeared into the house, and Dylan dragged his gaze back to the unfamiliar street stretching out before him. He unclenched his hands from the steering wheel and rolled up the window, wondering if he'd ever have the opportunity to play with his son. He brushed at his eyes that were tired and watery from his intense staring. And as he sat there, he made himself a promise that if he found his son, not a day would go by that he wasn't told how much he was loved.

It was nearing one when Dylan got to the hospital. He swung Chantal's door wide on silent hinges. She wasn't in bed. She stood, slightly bent over, at the window. He couldn't see what she was doing, but he had the feeling she was crying. He stepped through the door and saw that she was holding a pale yellow receiving blanket against her cheek. Her misery was like a knife to his heart. He knew that the memory of this moment would be with him until the day they put him six feet under.

A part of him wanted to go to her and offer whatever solace he could, but the part of him that was still bruised from her rejection whispered the reminder that she'd deliberately kept the knowledge of their son a secret from him. Without a sound, he turned and left her to her sorrow and went to try and find some ease for his own. Losing the son he'd wanted for so long was the worst thing that could possibly happen to him.

Wrong, Garvey. The worst thing that can happen is losing Chantal.

He pushed the taunting inner voice aside. Losing his child would be far worse than losing Chantal, he told himself, but the tiny voice whispered that he was fooling himself.

* * *

Dylan had his emotions well under control by the time one o'clock rolled around and the police artist arrived. Over the next two hours, by trial and error of putting facial features together, they came up with a drawing that Chantal said looked like the woman who'd taken her baby. Dylan sat through the afternoon, watching her, observing her grief and contributing little to the painstaking procedure.

By the time they were finished, she was pale with fatigue. Dylan wasn't feeling too great, either. Though he'd gone without sleep many times before, it never got easier. Shiloh rang Chantal's room at four and told him dinner would be ready at six-thirty, suggesting that he come out and grab a nap before the evening meal. Dylan didn't need any more encouragement and said he was on his way.

"The plantation isn't hard to find," Chantal told him.

"That's good, because I'm not sharp enough to unravel any mysteries this afternoon," he replied in a gruff tone.

"Don't be nervous. You'll enjoy staying with Cade and Shiloh."

He shot a glowering glance her way. "What makes you think I'm nervous?"

"Your shoulders are all drawn up and tight."

Dylan realized she was right. He rolled his shoulders and straightened. "I'm just tired."

"How long have you been up?"

"Almost thirty-six hours," he said, rubbing a palm over his whiskery cheek. "But I'm used to it."

"I don't see how anyone could get used to it." She lowered her gaze to the sheet and plucked at a wrinkle. "I want you to know that I appreciate your coming."

"Nothing could have kept me away." A combination of surprise and fear made her look up at him. "It's my child, too, Chantal. Mothers don't have a monopoly on love and concern."

"I never thought they did."

"No?" He folded the newspaper he'd bought and laid it on the bedside table. "I'll see you in the morning."

"You don't have to come tomorrow."

He shrugged. "I got nothin' else to do."

"What about helping the police?"

"The detective in charge said I was out of my jurisdiction."

"Have they found out anything?"

"Nothing. Other than your description, they don't have any leads. They're thinking that maybe this composite drawing of yours will jog some memories and get the ball rolling, so I hope you did a good job."

He could see the new doubts in her eyes. "So do I." She slammed her fist onto the mattress in frustration. Once. Twice. "Why didn't I pay more attention?" she cried, her eyes filling with tears that slipped down her pale cheeks.

Dylan circled her wrist in a strong but gentle grip. She tried to pull free. "Stop it!" he said in a taut, low voice. "Stop beating yourself up for something you have no control over." Surprised flickered in her eyes. "Do you think I don't know that you blame yourself for what happened?"

"H-how did you know?" she asked on a sob.

"Because that's the way it works." Without either of them being aware of it, his thumb began to rub a comforting circle over her narrow blue-veined wrist. "You're the one who turned the baby over to this crazy woman, so it's your fault. If one of the nurses had done it, you'd be blaming her, wouldn't you?"

She nodded. "How can you know that?"

"It's human nature," he said with a wry twist of his lips. "But you've got to put that notion out of our head. It's not your fault. It's no one's fault. The people who do these things are cagey. They've figured out all the angles. Believe me, there's no way you could have known she wasn't who and what she said she was."

"Maybe you're right," she said, "but it doesn't help much."

"Keep your chin up."

She nodded, but instead of raising her chin, she looked down at her wrist, manacled by his tan fingers. Awareness flared between them. Suddenly, Chantal uttered a mild curse.

Dylan released his hold on her. "What?"

Embarrassment stained her cheeks. "My milk..." she said helplessly. Dylan's gaze moved to her breasts. The front of her gown was wet and getting wetter. "I've been using a breast pump, but this still happens every now and then."

"Can I do something?" Dylan asked, concerned.

"You can get me a towel from the bathroom, please."

Dylan did as she asked. Chantal tucked the hand towel inside her gown. "They want me to start taking pills to dry up my milk,'' she said in a shaky voice. She raised her anguished gaze to Dylan's. ''But I can't do that. Not yet. If they find him, I want to be able to nurse him.''

Dylan felt as if a giant hand was squeezing his heart. As hard as it was for him, it must be doubly hard for her. He didn't know what to say.

She sank back against the pillows. ''The doctor told me that since I don't have any insurance, I can go home tomorrow, but I'm not sure I want to.''

''Why?''

Her eyes met his. ''I want to be here in case they find out something...or in case she...brings him back.''

Dylan didn't want to tell her that it was doubtful the woman would bring back the baby voluntarily, so he only addressed part of her concern. ''They can get the news to you at home as well as they can here.''

''Are you sure?''

''Positive.''

She offered him a wan, relieved smile. ''Thanks, Dylan.''

''For what?''

''For coming. For just...being here.''

Dylan felt an unaccountable pleasure growing inside him. For the first time in a long time he felt valued, needed. ''No problem.'' He smiled at her then, a quick, humorless quirk of his hard mouth that set her pulse to racing. ''See you tomorrow.''

Chapter Six

Dylan had no problem finding Magnolia Manor. His first glimpse of the plantation house relegated his weariness and his problems to the nether regions of his mind—at least for a moment. He sat at the end of the driveway and drank in the timeless beauty of the Greek Revival house set in the midst of a grove of magnolia trees—some only a few years old, some older than the house. He was awed by their size. Springtime at the plantation must be a fantastic sight.

At the back of the house were three small buildings that he assumed were the remaining slave quarters. A herd of Brangus heifers munched their way around the pasture, which was dotted with some sort of long-legged, white birds. Surprisingly, the cattle didn't seem to mind sharing their space. Beyond the spacious yard was the levee and the now-sluggishly moving bayou which had once floated every kind of boat imaginable.

History. He was looking at one of the few remaining pieces of a life-style that would never be again. For a guy who had grown up in a Chicago suburb it was an awesome feeling. As he watched, a large blue-gray bird took wing from some hidden place along the marshy edge of the bayou. Mesmerized by his surroundings and feeling his insignificance in the scheme of things, Dylan pulled into the driveway. He'd fit in here as comfortably as a prostitute in a nunnery.

Dylan got his suitcase and started up the brick walkway that led to the *galerie* circling the lower floor of the house. As if he'd been waiting for Dylan's arrival, Cade Robichaux stepped onto the porch, carrying a chubby, dark-haired baby wearing a red T-shirt and striped overall shorts. The baby was gnawing on his fingers; drool had drenched the bib around his neck and dripped down his arm to his dimpled elbow. Dylan wasn't prepared for the jolt of sadness that shot through him. He hadn't known that Chantal's brother had a baby...a son.

Cade met him at the top of the steps, his hand extended in greeting. "I see you found us. Welcome to Magnolia Manor."

The two men shook hands while the baby waved his dimpled fingers, gave a loud squeal and bestowed a wide smile on Dylan. Two tiny teeth made a brief appearance before the baby shoved his fist back into his mouth.

"Show-off!" Cade said with a laugh. "Dylan, meet my youngest and currently most spoiled son, Micah.

He gets his exhibitionist tendencies from his mother,"
he added, but Dylan heard the smile in his voice.

"Come on in." Dylan followed his host into the
house. He had the immediate impression of space,
antique furnishings, shiny floors and lace curtains,
that could be summed up in one word: class.

"I know you must be tired," Cade said, leading the
way to the stairs that were covered with a burgundy
runner held in place with brass strips. "Maybe you can
catch a nap before dinner."

"Sounds like a good idea," Dylan said. As if on
cue, the aroma of something cooking floated up the
stairs, setting his saliva glands to work.

Cade swung a door open and entered the room that
would be Dylan's for the night. A four-poster bed with
a fringed, crocheted canopy dominated the room,
which was painted a color that was something between forest green and dark teal. A Wedding Ring
quilt, softened with age, served as a bedspread. A
pristine white pitcher and basin had been placed on a
marble-topped washstand that resided nearby. A fluffy
white towel hung over the bar. A milk-glass vase sat on
an old trunk and held a bouquet of pink rambling
roses and trailing honeysuckle vine. The room was as
cheerful and friendly as Shiloh Robichaux.

"You can hang your things in here," Cade said,
opening the doors of an oak armoire that boasted
padded hangers and the elusive scent of lilac.

"Thanks," Dylan said, turning to take in the whole
room. "This place is fantastic."

"I got lucky," Cade told him. "When I bought it
two and a half years ago, it was being used as a hay
barn."

"You're kidding!"

"Nope," Cade said with a shake of his head. "Considering the state it was in, I bought it at a relatively reasonable price. I'd started the renovations, and when Shiloh and I got married, she helped me finish. We have compatible taste—thank goodness."

At the friendliness in Cade's voice, the last of Dylan's lingering uneasiness disappeared. Chantal's brother had a way of making a person feel right at home, yet Dylan knew he must be dying to know what was going on between him and his little sister.

Micah squealed again and stiffened in Cade's arms, a signal that he wanted down. Cade put him on the floor, and the baby made a beeline to a carved, white swan sitting beneath a window. Dylan had no idea babies could crawl so fast.

"How old is he?" he asked, unaware of the wistfulness in his voice and eyes.

"Eight months." Cade's mouth twisted. "I think I'm too old to go through all this again, but Shiloh assures me that running after Micah will keep me young." When Dylan shot him a questioning look, Cade explained. "I have an eighteen-year-old daughter and a son nearly twenty. Needless to say, they worship the ground Micah crawls on."

Both men glanced at the baby, who was using the swan to pull himself to his feet. The task accomplished, he looked up at his dad and gave him a wide smile that seemed to say, "I did it," and then promptly turned around, clamped both hands on the swan and started gnawing on the bird's head.

"Micah, don't chew on that," Cade commanded.

The baby let go of the swan and turned toward the stern command. Losing his precarious balance, he toppled over. The sound of his head hitting the floor coincided with his wail of pain.

Cade and Dylan both ran to the rescue, but Dylan got there first. Bending over, he gathered the warm, plump body close and cupped the back of Micah's head in his big hand. "You okay, big 'un?" he crooned into the baby's ear. "Huh? Where's it hurt?"

He sat down in an ancient rocker, put the baby on his knee and rubbed gentle, searching fingers over the softness of Micah's scalp. Sure enough, there was a goose egg behind his left ear.

Dylan looked up and met Cade's thoughtful gaze. "He's got a bump right here."

Cade squatted beside his son and took a look at his injury. "You'll live," he pronounced in a few seconds.

Micah held out his arms and Dylan relinquished the still-crying infant to his father. His arms felt strangely empty.

"Shh," Cade said, cuddling his son close. "It's all right." Micah's cries subsided to a hiccup and he ground his tiny fists into his tear-wet eyes. "Uh-huh. Just what I thought. You need a nap, kiddo."

There was a curious ache in Dylan's heart as he watched the exchange between father and son. He wondered if he'd ever have the opportunity to see his son's toothless smile or watch him take his falls while he learned about exploring and independence. He gave a harsh sigh that Cade mistook for weariness.

"Speaking of naps, let me get this monster out of here so you can get some rest," Cade said. He went to the door, Micah cradled in one arm. "I'll call you when dinner's ready."

"Great." Dylan watched with a bit of sorrow as they left the room. Then he pushed to his feet and kicked off his shoes. Not bothering to put away his clothes, he fell across the bed and stared sightlessly up at the ceiling. He felt as old as the house. Tired to the bone. Closing his weary eyes, he fell into the dreamless sleep that comes with total exhaustion.

It seemed like only a matter of minutes before there was a knock at the door and Cade poked his head in. Dylan pushed himself to one elbow.

"I hate to wake you, but dinner's in ten minutes."

Dylan cleared his throat and raked a hand through his tousled hair. "I'll be right down."

"The bathroom is at the end of the hall," Cade said.

"Thanks."

After brushing his teeth, shaving and combing his hair, Dylan felt somewhat fresher. The kitchen was easy to find; he just followed the tantalizing aromas wafting on the humid air that was moved through the house by ceiling fans suspended on long metal rods.

Though he was starving, he dreaded the prospect of making small talk with Chantal's family. Still, he'd never been accused of cowardice, so he squared his shoulders and entered the room with what he hoped passed for an eager smile on his face.

When he went back to his room an hour and a half later, he was surprised at how smoothly the meal of chicken-and-sausage gumbo and fresh-baked bread had gone. Talking to Shiloh and Cade was easy...

maybe because everyone had gone to great pains to steer the conversation away from personal topics. He'd heard the story about Magnolia Manor's history and how it was linked to nearby Rambler's Rest. He'd even found himself curious about the ghost that was supposed to haunt the Rambler plantation. He'd listened to Cade's rags-to-riches story and how he and Shiloh had met. Dylan was surprised to feel a pang of jealousy for the obvious happiness the Robichauxs shared.

Tired beyond belief, he'd declined their invitation to watch a movie on the VCR and had gone back upstairs to go to bed. He saw that Shiloh had turned back the sheets. The simple gesture brought an unexpected ache to his heart. No one had turned back his bed since he was a kid.

Damn! he chided himself, unzipping his suitcase. He was getting positively maudlin since he'd come to Louisiana. It must be something in that romantic, moisture-laden air. Smiling at his own fancifulness, he forced himself to unpack and hang his things in the armoire. Then he took a quick shower and crawled between the crisp, recently ironed cotton sheets. He was asleep in minutes, and didn't wake until the skinny fingers of morning sunlight pierced the leafy canopy of magnolia leaves outside his window and tickled him awake.

"You're right," Cade said when their guest had retired for the night.

"About what?"

"Dylan needing love. You should have seen him when Micah bumped his head. He got to him first, and even though he was awkward, I could tell he was concerned. And the look on his face..." Cade's voice trailed away. "I know he was thinking about his baby."

"Hmm. I know what you mean. I spent most of my time during dinner watching him watch the baby. He's hungry for that relationship. Maybe for any loving relationship." She was silent for long seconds. Finally, she asked, "What do you think happened between him and Chantal?"

"I don't have any idea, *chère*," Cade said, "but I'm damn well going to make it my business to find out."

Dylan woke to sunshine and bird song. After a country breakfast, Shiloh talked Cade into watching Micah while she went with Dylan to the hospital to bring Chantal back to Magnolia Manor to recuperate. The plan made sense to Dylan, but when they reached the hospital, Chantal had a different idea. She was packed up and ready to leave when they arrived.

"I'm not going to Magnolia Manor. I'm going back to my apartment."

"But you aren't able to take care of yourself yet," Shiloh said. "You're still weak from the surgery. You can't lift anything. Who's going to cook and take care of you?"

"Monique isn't far away. She'll keep a close watch on me. Besides, Gracie will be right downstairs. I'll be fine."

"That old harridan!" Shiloh muttered, though she adored Chantal's eccentric landlady. "I swear, you're as stubborn as your brother." She gathered up the previous day's newspaper and shoved it into the trash can beside the bed. "Look, when I lost my first baby, my mother came and stayed with me, and Molly came for three days when Micah was born, even though Cade was there. Let me tell you, it was nice having someone to help around the clock, someone who understood what I was going through. There's a lot to get used to, and—"

"Shiloh," Chantal interrupted, "I know you mean well, but I'll be fine. I mean, it isn't as if I have to worry about lifting the baby or anything."

Though they didn't need a reminder, mention of the baby not going home with her ushered a sudden uncomfortable silence into the room.

"I'll stay with her," Dylan said.

Shiloh watched Chantal's reaction; Chantal looked at Dylan. The thought of having him in her small apartment was frightening. He'd just be in the way. He'd be too close.... "I don't need you to take care of me."

"For once in your life, you're wrong, lady. I agree with Shiloh. You're not one hundred percent yet, and you have no business being alone right now." He shifted his weight to one leg, folded his arms over his chest and set his jaw. "You go home with Shiloh or I go home with you. It's your decision."

In the end, she agreed to let Dylan take her to the apartment, telling herself that Cade and Shiloh had done too much already, convincing herself that it would be okay to be alone with him. Under the circumstances, there wasn't much chance of anything happening between them, was there?

* * *

Chantal was embarrassed for Dylan to see her apartment, one of two on the upper level of a peeling, two-story farmhouse situated on five tree-studded acres at the edge of the city limits—too out of the way for most apartment dwellers. Currently, Chantal's neighbor was a retired teacher who spent most of the year visiting her various relatives.

Gracie Metcalf, the landlady, who lived on the bottom floor, was a retired Wac with the vocabulary of a longshoreman and the heart of a saint. Gracie was forever threatening to sell the "damned thing," claiming she was sick of the problems that went with renters.

The shotgun layout of Chantal's apartment, which she'd occupied for five years, consisted of a small kitchen and bath, a dining room, living room and a single bedroom. You could enter the living room via the front entry stairs, or the kitchen from the outside staircase. Chantal liked it because it was inexpensive, and it had a few architectural niceties that, in her opinion, lifted it above the ordinary: built-in china cabinets—which she'd spent days stripping down to the natural wood—situated on either side of the arched dining room opening, French doors leading to the bedroom, and an old-fashioned tub with claw feet. It had a lot of windows, which was a plus, and she loved the high ceilings and the wide trim.

She had furnished her home with inexpensive but nice odds and ends she'd picked up at garage sales and secondhand stores, and just before she'd lost her job, she'd painted and papered. Though small and ill arranged, the apartment was bright and cheerful, and it suited her. Shiloh and Cade claimed to love it, but she had doubts about Dylan's reaction to her humble abode. It was disconcerting enough to think that they'd made a child together, but that she didn't know much about his background or what he liked...except in bed...was even worse.

With a burdened heart, Chantal let Dylan help her out of the car. She felt she made the trek to the front door pretty well, even though she leaned on Dylan's arm the entire way. Though they went slowly, it was amazing how weak and light-headed she felt. By the time they reached the porch door, she was trembling.

Inside the front entry, Dylan looked up at the steep flight of stairs in disbelief. He uttered a curse. "You can't climb those."

"Of course I can," she said, and proceeded to try and do just that. She clung to the handrail and took one step and then two. Uncomfortable wasn't the word for the pain. It hurt like Hades. She paused and pushed a deep breath through her lips. She felt Dylan's hand on her shoulder and turned. Before she realized what he was doing, he eased her into his arms and carried her up the stairs.

Held close to his wide chest, Chantal was lost in a maelstrom of memories that were dangerous to her already-precarious state of mind—the forgotten strength of his arms, the familiar scent of his cologne, the way his hair curled over his collar in the back. When he set her down outside her door, it wasn't Dylan who was breathing hard. Their eyes met, but Chantal couldn't bear the intensity of his gaze, so she ducked her head and began to rummage in her purse for her old-fashioned skeleton key. Dylan took it from her, inserted it in the keyhole and swung the door wide.

Chantal stepped inside, thankful to be at home, even though the apartment had a stale, shut-up odor.

"It's like a furnace in here," Dylan said, crossing the room and opening the windows. "It should be aired out by the time I get you settled. Then we'll turn on the air-conditioning."

"Fine," Chantal said, heading for the bedroom. Just inside the bedroom door, she stopped. A small sob escaped her and she gripped his arm tighter. She'd forgotten all the preparations she'd made for the baby.

An antique cradle sat at the foot of the bed, but no baby would sleep in it tonight. A small white chest was crowded against the far wall, occupying space with a bookshelf and another chest painted forest green. A package of newborn diapers sat on its top, and a gaily decorated basket—a gift from Gracie—with a tired Mylar balloon tied to the handle was filled to overflowing with baby items.

She felt Dylan's arm slip around her shoulders and felt the touch of his hand as he skimmed it down her arm in a comforting gesture. She sagged against him and let her head fall against his chest.

"That's a great cradle. Where'd you find it?"

"Cade and Shiloh let me borrow it," she told him, a note of defeat ringing through her voice. "He found it in the attic at Magnolia Manor."

"It's incredible. The kid'll love it."

She tilted back her head and looked up at him. The steady determination burning in his eyes said she couldn't give in to her feelings of despair. He was right. They had to keep a positive, upbeat attitude. If they didn't, they would never make it through this. She straightened and squared her shoulders. Dylan's gaze moved to the rumpled bed.

"Where do you keep your linens?"

"In the middle drawer," she said, pointing to the green chest. She eased down into a floral print wing-back chair and watched as he deftly stripped and re-made the bed. "You're pretty good at that," she said as he tucked the pillow beneath his chin and drew on the pillowcase.

He shook the pillow sharply. "I've been single a long time." He turned back to one side of the bed. "Where are your gowns?"

"I don't wear gowns. My clean T-shirts are in the top drawer."

Dylan opened the drawer, drew out a Garfield T-shirt and carried it to her. "Can you manage by yourself?"

Chantal felt her cheeks grow warm. Was she blushing? Good grief, the man had seen her stark naked, had touched and kissed every inch of her. It was a lit-tle late for embarrassment. Nevertheless, the last thing she needed was Dylan's help.

He must have sensed her discomfiture. "You change. I'm going down to get your things out of the car. I'll be back in a minute."

"I'll be fine," she assured him.

Getting out of her clothes was harder than she ex-pected. She couldn't bend over, so she had to push the elastic-waist pants down her hips and let them slide to the floor. Her sandals and front-button shirt were easy to get off, but it wasn't fun raising her arms to get the T-shirt over her head. Still, by the time Dylan arrived with her suitcase, she was in bed, the sheet drawn up to her waist.

He brought in her flowers and placed them around the room, then he went to turn on the air-conditioning. She heard him in the kitchen getting ice, pouring a drink. Heard him in the bathroom. The sound of him moving around in her house was comforting, somehow. But then Dylan had always made her feel safe...even though she'd known he was trouble.

The scent of line-dried sheets filled her nostrils, and she let her thoughts drift back to the morning following the night they'd made love, the morning she had first realized just how dangerous Dylan Garvey really was....

Chantal awoke with a band of sunshine streaming across her face. She was in the Ramblers' antique sleigh bed, and Dylan lay sprawled beside her, one arm resting across her stomach. It was nice waking up next to someone. She'd forgotten just how nice.

She pushed the momentary pang away and reminded herself that she was in an extremely vulnerable position. More frightening than the depth of her desire and the completeness of her surrender the night before was the irrefutable fact that it was more than sex that drew her to Dylan Garvey, even though she was working overtime to convince herself that her feelings were nothing more than relief that he'd come to her when she needed help and comfort.

What was he feeling? she wondered. Neither of them had verbally expressed themselves the night before. For all she knew, he'd taken what she was so eager to give him simply because it was there for the taking. She knew something else: he was totally wrong for her. He seemed more like the love-'em-and-leave-'em type than the happily-ever-after type. But even knowing that he could walk out her door and never come back, she could find no trace of regret in her heart. Anything permanent between them was impossible, anyway. In less than three weeks, she would be back in Louisiana, and their time together would be no more than a sweet memory.

But she didn't want to think about that now. Chantal eased out from under his arm and slipped from the bed. After a brief shower, she pulled on clean underwear, slid her legs into some faded jeans, and topped her outfit off with a clean T-shirt that she tucked into her jeans. It was almost noon. She'd make them some breakfast and see what his attitude was when he got up. The main thing was to take things slow. She didn't want to listen to her conscience, which whispered that it was a little late for that.

She was breaking eggs into a bowl when he entered the kitchen, clad only in jeans he hadn't bothered to snap and a shirt he hadn't bothered to button. The sight of his partially bare chest and flat stomach set butterflies fluttering around in hers. She turned back to her task, a bemused expression on her face.

He put his arms around her and drew her against his hard warmth, pushing aside the heavy red brown swathe of her hair and kissing the side of her neck in a series of openmouthed kisses.

Her eyes drifted shut; her hands began to tremble. "Are you hungry?" she asked over her shoulder.

"Starving."

His hand moved to her breast. She could feel his hardness against her bottom and knew he wasn't talking about food. "So am I," she said, slipping from his grasp and taking a jug of juice from the refrigerator.

Dylan took the hint. A slight frown furrowed his forehead, but he made no move to push her. "Can I do anything to help?"

"You can set the table."

She was surprised at the efficient way he readied the table for their meal and impressed at the ease in which he kept the conversation going while they ate.

When the dishes were cleared and the dishwasher was loaded, he snapped his jeans and began to button his shirt. "I guess I should be going."

"Do you have to?" The question came as much as a shock to her as it did to him.

"I don't have to," he said, that intense gaze of his boring into her eyes. "I'd like nothing better than to spend the afternoon with you, but if I stay, I'm gonna want to make love to you, and I'm not sure that's what you want."

"Right now I'm not sure what I want," she told him honestly.

He took her hand in his and placed her palm against his chest. "You need some time."

She nodded.

"I know you're right. My mind says not to rush this, but the rest of me—" he carried her hand to the throbbing hardness of his arousal "—wants more."

Chantal sucked in a shallow breath. The idea of making love with him again was as exciting as it was frightening. "We can watch a movie."

"A movie." He raised his heavy eyebrows. "You want to watch a movie?"

"Not really. But I think we should."

They did. But the movie, an erotic thriller, did nothing to dampen the sexual tensions sizzling between them. When it was over, Chantal, who was lying on the sofa next to Dylan, felt as weak as a kitten. She was aware of her aching breasts, and the moisture gathering between her thighs.

"My turn," Dylan said. His voice was a deep rumble in her ear; his hand skimmed her hip.

"Your turn to what?" she asked, swinging her feet to the floor and tossing her long hair out of her face.

"My turn to pick something to do."

"Okay," she agreed. "I'm game for just about anything." As soon as the words left her lips, she realized that she had jumped feet first into uncharted, and possibly rough, seas.

"Anything?" he asked, his eyes dark with desire.

"Anything," she said on a sigh of defeat.

"Play cards with me."

Chantal blinked. "You want to play cards?"

He stood and took her cold hands in his. His gaze found her lips, lingered, then moved up to the question in her eyes. "Not just cards. Poker. Strip poker. We're in a gambling casino." He shrugged. "It seems fitting, somehow."

Chantal bowed to the inevitable. Dylan Garvey wasn't one to beat around the bush. He got right to the heart of the matter. And the truth was that she wanted him. More than she'd wanted a man in years.

"Okay," she said in a small voice. She started to go get the cards, but he caught her hand. Hooking his arm around her neck, he pulled her against him and took her mouth in a searing kiss. The touch of his lips kindled the flame that had been smoldering inside her ever since she'd awakened next to him.

He dragged his mouth free. "If you don't want to do this, you'd better tell me to go."

The warning was a harsh whisper muttered against her lips. There was anger in his voice, but she wasn't sure if he was angry with her for agreeing to his ridiculous scheme or with himself for suggesting it. "I can't," she said.

This time it was she who initiated the kiss. Again, it was he who ended it. "Go get the cards," he said in a voice that was far from steady.

As they settled down on the floor in front of the fireplace, Chantal found herself wondering why they were bothering to go through the motions. Playing strip poker was unnecessary, a farce with no purpose. They both knew how the game would end. On second thought, maybe it did have a purpose. Instead of falling into bed at the demand of their raging hormones, playing the game would give them both time to think about what they were about to do, time for her to reconsider and back out if she wanted.

It would also prolong the anticipation, even though she wasn't sure she could stand much more. Need flowed through her body, igniting fires in every molecule along the way. Cards in hand, she knelt in front of Dylan, who sat cross-legged in front of the roaring fire.

"Five card stud?" she asked, recalling the game from her childhood when she and Cade and Monique had played for kitchen matches.

"Suits me."

Dylan cut the deck, and she dealt the first round of cards. There was no need for money or chips. The outcome would depend on the luck of the draw, not skill and bluffing. At the end of the hand—which she won—Dylan shrugged philosophically, unbuttoned his shirt, peeled it off and tossed it in the direction of the sofa.

The display of utter masculinity sent Chantal into what her mama would have called a regular tizzy. Before she dropped her gaze to the cards, she got a glimpse of sharply defined musculature, a hard middle, and dark nipples peeking from whorls of even darker chest hair. It was a sight she recalled well from the night before, one she was certain would always evoke this aching, empty feeling inside her.

Dylan reached over and took the cards from her numb fingers. She was so caught up in her thoughts that she wasn't aware of the cards he dealt her or how she was playing them until he said, "Take off your top."

"What!"

The look in his eyes was as hot as Louisiana on the Fourth of July. "You lost that hand, baby. Sorry."

She looked at her cards. He was right. Casting a quick look at him, she grasped the bottom of her T-shirt. Telling herself that she had swimsuits that covered less, she took a deep breath and whipped the soft knit over her head.

Dylan muttered a low curse. Seeing the direction of his gaze, Chantal realized she was wearing a push-up bra. Creamy mounds of upthrust flesh looked as if they were on the verge of spilling over the gossamer lace that did nothing to cover her nipples, puckered now beneath the heat of his gaze.

The knowledge that she could affect him so strongly was both an aphrodisiac and a much-needed shot to her self-esteem. She felt sexy and pretty and as nervous as she had on her first date. Struggling for a composure she was far from feeling, she lifted her chin and held out her hand.

He slapped the cards into her palm. "This was a very bad idea," he said in a tight voice.

"What's the matter, Garvey?" she said in a tough-girl tone that hid her nervousness. "No one ever call your bluff before?"

"Just deal."

She did and she lost. The look on Dylan's face was something between anticipation and a bad-natured scowl. Recanting the swimsuit theory and determined not to act like a prissy old maid, she stood and unfastened her jeans. The downward slide of the zipper filled the stillness of the room. Watching for his reaction, she hooked her thumbs in the waistband and pushed the denim down. There was no sense prolonging the agony.

And agony was exactly what it was beginning to be. Every time his eyes made a lingering survey of her body, she thought she would die with wanting. She wasn't sure she could stand it if he touched her. She wasn't sure she could stand it if he didn't.

She peeled the jeans off and sat down, clasping her arms around her updrawn knees to guard her body from the blatant desire in his eyes.

"I have a photographic memory," he said, a devilish twinkle in his eyes.

"Just stop the harassment and deal," she said, "or you're gonna be sorry."

"Hell," he said in resignation, "I'm gonna be sorry, anyway." He flipped her a card.

His confession of having second thoughts erased her embarrassment. "If you're going to regret it, let's stop this right now."

"That's my line," he said in a grim voice. "I couldn't stop now if my life depended on it, so don't get any ideas about pulling out at the last minute." He slid a card from the deck. "Last card coming up."

She looked at her hand and sighed.

"What do you have?"

She held up four cards. "Two pair. Queens high. And I wouldn't dream of pulling out, Mr. Garvey."

"That's real good, because I have three tens, and you lose again."

A blank look settled on Chantal's face. "But... that's not fair. You're still dressed."

"What can I say? I'm a lucky kind of guy."

Her teeth sank into the softness of her lower lip. Setting her chin at a lofty angle, she lowered her knees and reached up to undo the front clasp of her bra.

"Let me help you."

The soft entreaty brought her gaze to his. A growing desire glimmered in their depths. Laying the cards aside, he knelt in front of Chantal and drew her to her knees.

In a gesture that was fast becoming familiar, he cradled her face in his hands. She was drowning in the passion in his eyes, sinking unresistingly into the need that was towing her under. Her hands went to his shoulders and slid down his upper arms to his elbows and back again. His skin was warm and sleek over the firmness of the muscles beneath. Unable to stop herself, she moved her palms to his chest, working her fingers through the silky hair growing there, finding his flat nipples and rubbing them with soft, concentric circles.

Dylan growled deep in his throat and trailed a series of rough, openmouthed kisses to her ear and the side of her neck. His hands skimmed beneath her wispy underwear, cupping the roundness of her bottom and pulling her into the vee of his legs. She could feel the roughness of his jeans and the undeniable hardness of his arousal pressing against her.

Leaning back, she shook her hair away from her face. Her eyes locked with Dylan's, who reached out and freed the front clasp of her bra with a flick of his thumb. He lowered his head and touched his tongue to her breast in a caress so soft she might have imagined it. But when he drew the nipple into his mouth there was no denying the exquisite pleasure that spiraled through her. Dylan eased her to the rug and lowered himself beside her.

Closing her eyes with a quiescent sigh, she gave herself over to the kaleidoscope of emotions shifting through her as he rid her of her last piece of clothing. This time there was no desperation to their lovemaking. This time there was time and inclination to savor each touch, each kiss.

Adrift on a sea of sensation, she felt him move and moaned at the sudden cessation of warmth. Her ears noted the rustle of denim when he took off his jeans. The air she breathed was redolent with the scent of cologne and deodorant and man. She tasted the cool mint of his breath as his mouth plundered hers in a series of mind-drugging, soul-shattering kisses. She reveled in the strength of his arms and the hardness of his desire as he lowered his body between her thighs.

She felt his hand between their bodies and whimpered in pleasure against his mouth. Feeling a firm pressure against the juncture of her thighs, she lay still and quivering. When Dylan started to draw away she clutched at his shoulders. "Don't stop."

"Are you sure?"

Chantal nodded. But she wasn't sure of anything except that if he stopped, she would die. It was only later, when she found out that he'd lied about who he was and what he did that the doubts began to creep in. But by then, it was too late to do more than try to piece together the torn fabric of her life.

Chapter Seven

When Dylan got all of Chantal's things put away and went to check on her, he found she had fallen asleep. Closing the French doors to block any noise he might make, he spent the next hour and a half picking up, dusting, running the carpet sweeper and taking out the trash. With nothing else to do, he turned on the TV and was soon watching an old Western. He was dozing when someone knocked on the kitchen door. Stifling a yawn, he made his way through the apartment and opened the back door. A woman stood there, a casserole in her mitted hands and a cigarette dangling from her thin lips.

The visitor was no more than five foot two inches. She had a wiry build, and Dylan doubted she weighed a hundred pounds sopping wet. If the lines around her eyes and mouth were anything to go by, he judged her to be in her sixties—her late sixties. Her iron gray hair was cut in a fashionable short style, and she wore high-top sneakers, baggy army green walking shorts that exposed her knobby knees, and a matching ribbed tank top that drew attention to her protruding collarbones. She looked as hard as nails.

"You must be the father," she said, speaking around the cigarette as she brushed past him into the kitchen.

So much for introductions. He watched with a bemused expression as she set the ground beef and tortilla dish on the stove, pulled off one kitchen mitt and removed the cigarette from her lips. "I brought your supper."

"Thanks," he acknowledged with a nod. "You're right. I'm the father, Dylan Garvey. And you must be—"

"The landlady—Gracie Metcalf." She flipped her ash into the sink, careful to see that it fell into the drain. Leaning a scrawny hip against the cabinet, she said, "So what finally brings you here?"

Dylan wondered if he imagined the emphasis she placed on "finally." He didn't think so. Who the hell did the old bat think she was, anyway, questioning him as if he were the prime suspect in some heinous crime?

"Nobody invited me until yesterday," he said, the look in his eyes as challenging as hers.

Gracie's jaded gaze meandered from his feet to his narrowed eyes. "I don't doubt it," she said at last. "But then, again, I can't say as I blame her, either. You're a hard case, aren't you, Mr. Garvey?"

"It takes one to know one . . . ma'am," he said.

Instead of taking offense, Gracie Metcalf began to laugh, a hoarse cackling that sent her into a fit of coughing. Dylan was getting worried, when she managed to get the hacking under control. She looked at the cigarette and held it aloft with a considering expression. "I gotta stop smokin' these things. Doc says they're gonna kill me." Then she turned on the tap, stuck the cigarette under the water and tossed it into the trash can beneath the sink.

"So how's our girl?" she asked, jerking her head in the direction of the bedroom.

"As well as can be expected." Dylan looked into Gracie's uncompromising pale blue eyes. "Actually, I don't think she's up to much at this point, but she'll never admit it."

Gracie nodded. "She's as independent as they come and darn good at hidin' how she really feels, cause she's scared of gettin' hurt." While Dylan was thinking about that, she crossed her arms over her meager breasts. "So what's your story? Why'd you take so long to come?"

"I already told you. I didn't get called until yesterday."

Gracie's eyebrows lifted in disbelief. "Are you tryin' to tell me that you just found out about the baby yesterday?"

"You got it."

Gracie chewed on that awhile. "So what happened between the two of you—besides the obvious, I mean?"

"Chantal didn't think we had any future. We're too different. And she thought I lied to her."

"Did you?"

For the life of him, Dylan couldn't figure out why he was letting this skinny old crow put him through the third degree. Maybe it was because, in spite of her gruff way, he sensed that she truly cared about Chantal.

"No. I was working undercover and couldn't tell her who I really was. She didn't think that was a good enough excuse."

"Undercover? So you're a cop, huh?"

"That's right."

"Are you any good—undercover, I mean?" she asked with a grin.

Good Lord. Was she flirting with him? "I like to think so."

"And our girl thought you should have told her the truth despite the fact that you were working?" She shook her head. "Sounds like her. Hardheaded as all get out. But it proves my point. She's afraid of gettin' hurt." Before Dylan could reply, she asked, "Have they found out anything about the baby yet?"

"No."

"They will." She pushed away from the cabinets. "So, is there anything I can do for you, Dylan Garvey?"

"You wouldn't want to stay with Chantal a couple of hours while I take the composite picture around the hospital, would you?"

"I'd be glad to." She showed her teeth again. "Dyin' to get in the thick of it, aren't you?"

Dylan's return smile was quick, almost guilty. "I want to find my baby, yeah."

"'Course I'll stay," Gracie said. "Do me a favor, will you?"

"Sure."

"Pick me up a carton of cigarettes while you're gone."

Dylan pulled in front of the house two hours later, tired and discouraged. No one at the hospital had seen the woman in the drawing, and since the cops had already made one round, they were a little ticked off at being questioned again. One nurse thought the picture looked familiar, but no, she couldn't say she'd actually seen the woman in the drawing on the hospital premises.

He struck the steering wheel with his palm. Damn! He hated telling Chantal his search had been fruitless. With his shoulders slumped, he got out of the car and made his way up the steps to the apartment. He found Chantal sitting at the kitchen table drinking coffee while Gracie worked at putting together a salad. Two loaves of homemade bread sat rising on the stove, and a pot of coffee gave off a heartening aroma.

The kitchen was small, but Chantal had done wonders with it. The floor was covered in white-and-black tile. The room was predominately white, but green plants on a red metal baker's rack and red Formica on the cabinet top added the pizzazz the small room needed. With the tantalizing scents teasing his nostrils and the bright white, green and red color scheme warming his senses, Dylan couldn't shake the feeling that he'd come home.

"Hi," Chantal said, tucking a strand of hair behind her ear. "Any luck?"

He hated to dash the faint ray of hope in her eyes. "No. I'm sorry."

"It isn't your fault," she said, repeating the words he'd said to her the day before.

He nodded and put Gracie's cigarettes on the table. "These okay? I forgot to ask what brand you smoked."

"Long as they got nicotine in 'em, they'll do," she said. "How 'bout a cup of coffee?"

"Sounds great." He sat down next to Chantal at the small table that was draped with a white tablecloth bearing splashes of bright red geraniums that echoed the plants sitting on the sunny sill above the sink. "Two spoonfuls of sugar, please."

"Hell, boy, I ain't your servant," Gracie said, plunking the mug of coffee and the sugar bowl down in front of him.

Dylan was too tired to be angry. Besides, there was something about the feisty old woman he liked. He gave her a wan smile. "A nineties lady, are you, Gracie?"

"I was a nineties lady in the forties, boy. Joined the service during the war when everyone said it was a man's world, a man's war. I did my part, and I was good at it, too. Damn good."

"I don't doubt it," he said, measuring out his sugar and stirring it into the dark brew. He lifted it to his lips and took a big mouthful. His eyes began to water; it was all he could do to force the liquid down. He set down the mug and gave a mighty shudder. "This coffee has chicory in it."

The comment was more accusation than a statement.

"I know that, son," Gracie said, using the same placating tone she might use when talking to someone a tad slow. "I made it."

"Does anyone around here make real coffee?"

"*This* is real coffee," she said, tapping the rim of the cup with a bony finger. "Now, drink it up, boy. It'll put hair on your chest."

"He already has hair on his chest," Chantal said.

Dylan's eyes met hers. The blush coloring her face told him she remembered a lot more than the hair on his chest, but at least her embarrassment temporarily rid her eyes of sorrow.

"Try some milk in it," Chantal said, attempting to steer the conversation back to neutral territory. "Maybe you can get it down that way."

It did help. Dylan even managed to drink a second cup with his dinner, which Gracie shared with them, at Chantal's insistence. The salad was crisp, but as a meat-and-potatoes man, he found the casserole just passable. But the bread was to die for. He lost count of how many slices he had. Glowing beneath his praises, Gracie promised to show him how to make it. Dylan was a little saddened by the thought that he wouldn't be around long enough to learn.

When they finished eating, he helped Chantal up from the table. Even though she could move slowly, it was obvious that she was still in a great deal of discomfort.

"Are you okay?"

"Yeah," she said, straightening to her full height even though he could tell it was painful. "Just sore. Can you help me to the bathroom?"

"Sure."

"Thanks. I can tell I'm getting stronger, but I'm still a little shaky."

Dylan left her outside the bathroom, instructed her to call when she was finished and went to see if Gracie needed help cleaning up the kitchen. The old woman told him to "take care of our girl," and Dylan prowled the small living room until he heard the bathroom door open.

He offered Chantal his arm. "Do you want to go back to bed?"

"I'm sick of bed," she told him. "I think I'll try to sit up and watch a little TV."

Dylan helped her to the living room and watched as she eased herself into one corner of the sofa. Halfway down she gave a sharp little cry that pierced the softening exterior of his hard heart.

"What's the matter?"

The taut question brought her eyes up to his. "I just twisted a little the wrong way or something. I'm okay."

Dylan searched her face for signs that she was just pretending to be all right and, finding none, tried to force his heartbeats to a normal rhythm. He sat down next to her. "Is it pretty bad?" he asked, wanting—needing—to know, even though he hadn't meant to discuss the baby with her.

She gave him a lopsided smile. "Well, major surgery is never pleasant, but I feel better every day."

"Cade said you had to have the C section because the baby was so big."

"Nine pounds and one ounce," she said. "I was in labor about fifteen hours."

Imagining her lying in some hospital bed alone, hurting, Dylan swore softly. He'd never dreamed that the time they spent together would cause her that kind of pain.

"I started taking the pills today," she said. He heard the tension in her voice.

"What pills?"

"The ones to dry up my milk. My doctor said that under the circumstances, he thought it was the best thing."

Physically, maybe. But mentally, Dylan could tell the decision was eating at her. Unable to think of anything that would comfort her, he did the best he could. "Speaking of doctors... I heard you say you didn't have any insurance. I don't want you worrying about it. I'll take care of your medical bills."

"You don't have to do that," she said stiffly.

"I want to. It's the least I can do." His troubled gaze met hers. From what she'd told him in Atlantic City, she'd been through hell the last year or so, working at part-time jobs and wondering how she was going to make ends meet. Then, to experience major surgery because he'd gotten her pregnant... "I should have been here."

"I see that now," she said dropping her gaze to her hands which were twined in her lap. "You had a right to know. I have no excuse except that I was scared... and selfish." Two fat tears rolled down her cheeks, and she reached up to brush them away. "I'm sorry."

Seeing the tears trickle down her cheeks brought a now-familiar ache to his heart. Hearing her admit she was wrong didn't bring the pleasure he imagined it would. He felt as if opposing armies waged a battle inside him, and his soul would go to the victor. He didn't understand how he could feel such misery in the face of her pain and still be so angry with her for what her selfishness had cost him, what it had cost them both.

But even though a part of him blamed her, he wanted to reach out, pull her into his arms and kiss the tears away. He wanted to tell her that everything would be all right, that they'd find their son, that he'd go to hell and back to find him.

"I want my baby," Chantal moaned, burying her face in her hands. Dylan's fingers clenched in his lap. He opened his mouth to say something, but no words found their way to his lips. His own pain was eating him up from the inside out. He thought of the night Chantal had sought comfort in his arms, the first time they'd made love. He remembered what Carole had told him about women needing comfort, someone to hold them. Well, men needed that, too. He needed it right now. He wanted to find solace in her arms, to hear her murmur those stereotypical platitudes and have her reassure him that everything was going to be all right.

But what about Chantal? Did she need those things? She claimed she didn't need him or any man, and just today she'd informed him that she didn't need him doing anything for her. Did that include offering her comfort? On the heels of those troubling thoughts came a memory of himself as a child, reaching out to his dad and being pushed aside.

Chantal drew a deep, shuddering sob, and he leaped to his feet. Hell, he didn't even know what to do to ease his own pain much less hers, and one thing was certain: he couldn't bear offering her solace in his arms and having her turn him away.

Muttering a curse, Dylan turned on his heel and went to the door.

"Where you goin'?" Gracie called from the kitchen.

"Out," he said, and shut the door quietly behind him.

He was leaving! Chantal watched the door close with disbelief. She must have made him angry by talking about the baby, but he was the one who'd instigated the conversation, and she'd felt it was time for them to declare some sort of truce, if not for themselves, for their child.

For a while there, she'd thought he was softening toward her. She hadn't mistaken the empathy emanating from him, and there was something in his eyes she'd never seen before. It wasn't anger, or that cocky confidence that was so much a part of him. It wasn't the heat of desire. It was anxiety, concern for her.

Gracie came out of the kitchen, drying her hands on a dish towel. "Where'd our boy go?"

Chantal sniffed and wiped at her damp cheeks with the back of her hand. "I don't know."

"Well, when he comes back, you be extra nice to him. He's hurtin' as bad as you are."

Chantal looked up sharply. "Well, he certainly has a strange way of showing it."

"That's because he's a lot like you."

She and Dylan alike? No way. "You're wrong, Gracie. Dylan Garvey and I are nothing alike. He's distant and uncommunicative. I never know what he's thinking . . . or feeling."

Gracie laughed, that full-bodied laughter that set her to coughing again. When she had the spasm under control, she wiped her eyes and wheezed, "That's exactly the way you are until a body gets to know you. Your Dylan's an independent cuss—just like you. Too proud to admit he needs anyone or anything."

"What makes you think that?"

"I know because we're three of a kind," Gracie said sagely, "and like Dylan says, it takes one to know one."

Afraid he'd wake Chantal, Dylan was careful to be quiet when he let himself into the apartment. Sure enough, she was asleep. A pillow, a set of sheets and a summer-weight blanket lay at one end of the sofa, which looked about two feet too short. He sighed and began to make up his bed. Then he showered, pulled on some running shorts and stretched out on the sofa as best he could. As he expected, it was too short, but he was so tired it probably wouldn't make any difference.

He reached up and switched off the reading lamp Chantal had left on for him and closed his eyes. As weary as he was, his mind replayed every scrap of conversation, every nuance of emotion he'd seen reflected in her eyes during their earlier conversation. An hour later, he was still awake, turning from side to side on the narrow sofa, punching his pillow with all the force he used on the punching bag at his favorite gym, and swearing softly into the darkness.

He thought about Chantal so sound asleep in the other room. He thought about the extra length of her queen-size bed and remembered the way he'd awak-

ened in the night in Atlantic City to find her burrowed up against his chest. Damn! He didn't need
erotic memories on top of everything else! He rolled
onto his back, threw his arm over his face and tried
counting sheep. That didn't work, either. Telling
himself he was probably digging himself a hole he'd
never be able to crawl out of, he got up and headed to
Chantal's bedroom. They'd slept together once, what
could it hurt now?

Brightness from a security lamp outside insinuated
itself between the small cracks in the blinds, casting
minimal light into the darkened room and silhouet-
ting Chantal's body. He tiptoed across the room and
around the foot of the bed. Being careful not to make
a sound, he pulled back the sheet and eased himself
down onto the mattress in slow increments. She didn't
stir. He sighed in relief and, lacing his fingers together over his middle, allowed himself to relax against
the cool sheets. They were crisp against his flesh and
smelled of fabric softener and sunshine, the same scent
that had clung to Chantal's T-shirt.

His lips quirked in the darkness at the memory of
her T-shirt wardrobe. She wasn't the satin-and-lace
type, though she'd looked damn good in the finery
she'd worn at Rambler's when they first met. No, she
was the T-shirt type, and the thrust of her breasts and
the way the skimpy length displayed her long legs did
more for the everyday apparel than any slogan or logo
ever designed.

Thinking about her bare legs and the way her
breasts looked beneath the soft cotton made Dylan
acutely aware that it had been a long time since he'd
had a woman, a long time since he'd made love with

Chantal. Cautiously, he raised himself to one elbow and stared at her sleeping form in the darkness, wondering what would happen when they found the baby—or worse—what would happen if they didn't.

If he found the baby, would Chantal agree to let him be a part of his son's life? And how could he do that if he lived in New Jersey? He supposed he could move to Louisiana. He liked the scenery, the people and even the muggy heat. He certainly wasn't in love with Atlantic City. He'd only moved there because Carole wanted to be near her family. He'd stayed after the divorce because he had no close ties to anyone or any-place else.

That was different now. He had family now. A son. And he intended to be a part of his life.

What if you don't find him? What will you do then, Dylan? Go back to being a lonely, bitter man? And what about Chantal? What will happen to her?

Dylan reclined against the pillow once more, pushing the troubling thoughts from his mind. He refused to think negatively. He couldn't afford to. They would find the baby. *He* would find him if he had to knock on the doors of every house in the state.

Some noise awakened her. Instantly awake, Chantal's eyes flew open and encountered darkness. Fear made her mouth dry and caused her heartbeats to quicken. There it was again, a soft whooshing sound...like breathing. Someone was in the room with her! Careful not to move too fast, she turned her head and saw that that someone was not only in her room, but in her bed! From the corner of her eye, she could see the darkened outline of a massive shoulder rising from the place next to her. She was about to panic when she caught a whiff of men's cologne. The scent was one she'd become intimate with during the time she'd been in New Jersey. She felt her body go limp with relief. It was Dylan lying next to her, not some prowler... or some pervert, which she should have realized. Dylan would never let an intruder get into the house... much less her bed.

"Dylan?" she queried softly in the darkness.

"Hmm?

"What are you doing in here?" The question was a harsh whisper. Dylan didn't seem to notice.

"Trying to sleep," he mumbled.

"You're supposed to sleep on the sofa."

"It's too short."

"But—"

"Can't we talk about this in the morning?" he asked, his voice tempered with exasperation and thick with sleepiness. "I'm tired."

The question had the desired effect. She recalled the many times she'd fallen asleep on the sofa. Remembering what it had done to her back, she had to admit she couldn't blame him.

C'mon, Chantal! What will it hurt?

Nothing, she assured herself, even as her body filled with a new tension, one engendered by the masculine form lying so close to her. She told herself that sharing a bed with Dylan was no big deal—after all, it wasn't as if they'd never shared one before. Besides, it was obvious that even if she hadn't just had a baby, intimacy was the furthest thing from Dylan's mind.

Still, it felt intimate, lying next to him, the even sounds of his breathing a sweet lullaby falling on her ears. It felt...nice. As usual when Dylan was around, she felt safe, as if things would take care of themselves. Chantal closed her eyes and made a decision. She didn't know how she would face him the next day, but she didn't have the heart to make him leave, especially with Gracie's reminder that he was suffering, too, ringing in her ears. Right now, she planned to go back to sleep. She'd worry about whatever awkwardness she might feel tomorrow.

Dylan woke just as the sun was coming up, thankful to see that Chantal was still asleep. He eased himself from the bed and padded silently back to the living room, where he took a pair of clean jeans from the small coat closet. He tugged them on and went into the kitchen to put on the coffee. He grimaced when all he saw was the god-awful chicory brew the south Louisianians seemed to favor. He'd forgotten to get some plain old ordinary coffee.

As he measured out what he hoped was the prescribed amount of dark-roasted grinds, he couldn't help the slight smile that hovered on his lips. He wasn't sure he could pull it off two nights in a row, but he'd managed to get a decent night's sleep in Chantal's bed without going to battle over it.

He was lifting some charred bacon out of the skillet when he saw her coming out of the bedroom. She carried some clothes over her arm.

"Need any help?"

"I can do it, thanks," she said, pushing a tousled swath of hair from her face as she headed for the bathroom.

"Don't lock the bathroom door."

She stopped in her tracks. "What?"

"Gracie says you shouldn't lock the bathroom door. That way, if you faint or something, I can get in to help you."

"I'm not going to faint," she said testily.

Dylan searched her face for any indication that she was angry about his climbing into her bed and found none. "Humor me."

She nodded. "Okay, I won't lock the door." Her voice dripped sarcasm.

"Thank you."

He knew she was feeling better when she came out of the bathroom fully dressed and wearing makeup. Her long chestnut hair was caught back in a ponytail that accentuated the exotic sweep of her cheekbones. If not for the haunted look lurking in her eyes, the style would have made her look more like a little girl than a thirty-six-year-old woman. Though she was still careful about sudden movements, she was walking more freely. There was no doubt she was on the mend.

Without Gracie there to act as a buffer, breakfast conversation was sparse. Dylan felt that their talk the day before had taken them across some imaginary boundary into a land of no return. They were at an impasse; neither of them was sure how or where to proceed from there.

Out of a sense of guilt for what he'd unwittingly put her through and the desire to help, he'd offered her money; she'd misunderstood, seeing his action as some sort of charity. When he'd commented that he should have been here for the baby's birth, he'd meant that he should have been there to support her. Chantal thought he was still harping about her not telling him about the baby.

Once again, he'd failed to communicate his true feelings. Once again, he'd failed to give a woman what she needed. No wonder there were so many divorces, he thought. Men and women didn't even speak the same language.

He knew he hadn't helped their situation when he'd walked out, leaving her alone with her misery. He could offer her no explanation for his leaving. No excuses. All he knew was that he'd reverted to the same behavior he'd used during his marriage, simply because he didn't know what else to do.

And because he was afraid.

Seeing her sitting there, her heart breaking, he'd felt a powerful desire to go to her and put his arms around her. Fear had sent him out the door. Gut-deep fear that she would reject his overture of comfort the way she had his offer of money.

The light of a new day hadn't brought any change in their circumstances. He knew that uncertainty and a feeling of helplessness was eroding his usual confidence, which made him a bit short-tempered. The feeling of frustration that hung over them and the confusion he was experiencing in his feelings for Chantal weren't helped by the fact that he found it harder and harder to work up any anger toward her. Even now, he found himself wanting to pull the elastic band off her hair, tangle his hands in its luxuriant softness and drag her mouth to his.

The mental image didn't do much to improve his frame of mind. He was softening toward her, and that was dangerous. He had to keep himself centered on finding the baby and forget the passion they'd shared. Chantal had caught him with his guard down once, and he couldn't allow it to happen a second time.

They finished breakfast and he did the dishes while Chantal read a book called *You and Your Newborn*. Throughout the morning she chatted with several friends who called. He washed a load of clothes and perused the paper from front page to last. He even read two copies of *Better Homes and Gardens*. By noon, he was pacing the floor. After lunch, Chantal took a nap, and, in desperation, he got out the phone book and dialed the police department.

"Detective Rousseau? Hi. This is Dylan Garvey."

"Mr. Garvey. What can I do for you?" the policeman asked, though there could be no doubt about why Dylan was calling.

"Have you found out anything?"

"Nothing yet. By the way, I hear you made a sweep through the hospital yesterday afternoon with the composite drawing."

"Yeah, I did."

"I thought we agreed that you're out of your jurisdiction."

"We did." Dylan scraped a hand through his hair in a distracted gesture. "I didn't claim I was connected to any police department. I asked as a father trying to locate his child. Is there a law against that?"

"No, but—"

"But you don't want me butting in and screwing up your investigation."

"Right."

Dylan gave a sigh of frustration. "So have you checked out the hospital records to see what women lost babies yet?"

"Not yet, but we will." There was no hiding the growing irritation in Rousseau's voice.

"When?" Dylan prodded.

"When I get the manpower, damn it!" Rousseau barked. "Now get off my back."

Dylan realized he was being unreasonable. He let out a slow, harsh breath. "Look, I'm sorry. I'm outta line. It's just that I'm getting worried. The baby's mother is holding herself together by the grace of God. And you know as well as I do that the more time that passes, the colder the leads get."

It was Rousseau's turn to sigh. "You aren't telling me anything I don't already know. Look, will it make you happy if I pull one of my patrolmen off the street to start checking the hospital records?"

"It wouldn't make me happy, Detective Rousseau," Dylan said with a fleeting grin. "It would make me ecstatic."

"I'll get someone over there within the hour."

"Thanks. You don't know how much I appreciate it."

"You'd better," Rousseau said, and hung up.

Dylan didn't even mind that the detective didn't bother with a goodbye. At least he had something positive to tell Chantal.

Encouraged, he started calling every family counselor and psychologist who practiced in Thibodaux and the surrounding area, explaining who he was and asking if any of them might be treating a woman with mental problems that could be tied to the loss of a child or the inability to conceive or carry a baby.

In every case, the receptionist was very close-mouthed. As soon as they ascertained that he was not with the local police, they told him they were sorry, but the information was confidential. One was gracious enough to say that if he cared to make an appointment, the doctor might talk to him. Discouraged, Dylan hung up. As in his relationship with Chantal, he seemed to have taken one step forward with Rousseau's promise to check the hospital records and two steps back with his luck in pumping the local shrinks for information.

Chapter Eight

Somehow, they made it through the day. Gracie stopped by, but even though Chantal could tell Dylan was going stir-crazy, he didn't ask the landlady to stay with her again. She was glad. Even though they hadn't talked much, his nearness was somehow comforting. He fixed tomato soup and grilled cheese for their evening meal and managed to scorch them both. She tucked it away without complaint. Like her, he was doing his best to cope with a bad situation.

As she watched Dylan pick at his dinner she realized Gracie was right: he held too much inside. He was hurting. Badly. As badly as she. Chantal wasn't sure how she knew that, she only knew she did. Oh, he put up a good front, but there were moments she caught him off guard and saw the pain reflected in his dark eyes. It was all she could do to stop herself from going to him and drawing his dark head to her breasts, to offer him the same comfort she wanted so badly to find in his arms.

"Don't feel as if you have to stay here with me every minute," she said at last. "Monique is coming over for the afternoon."

Dylan looked up from his soup. "What do you mean?"

"Staying cooped up here with me is driving you crazy. I know you'd rather be doing something to help find the baby."

"Rousseau won't let me do anything." His hard mouth twisted into a semblance of a smile. "Besides, my dad would say that this is what builds character."

"What? Staying in a house with a sick woman all day?"

"No. Doing anything you don't want to do."

She felt the hot color rise in her face and saw it rise in his. "I don't mean to be a burden to you."

"I didn't mean you—or this situation in particular," Dylan hastened to explain, an abashed look on his face. "I just meant that that was his basic philosophy about life."

Chantal thought about his ability to separate himself from things, thought about his innate toughness. Had he been born that way, or had he learned it from his father just as she'd learned her first lesson in not trusting people from hers?

"Did you have to do a lot of things you didn't want to?" she asked, not knowing if he'd answer or tell her to mind her own business.

A genuine smile curved Dylan's lips, revealing his straight white teeth and carving twin grooves in his lean cheeks. As she tried to regain control of her galloping heartbeats Chantal found herself thinking that maybe it was a blessing he didn't smile more often. As far as her heart went, his smile could be considered a lethal weapon.

"Let's just say that if I had any more character I'd be a candidate for sainthood."

The comment brought a smile to her lips. It was as close as he'd ever come to revealing he had any sense of humor. "What about your mother? What did she contribute?"

"What love she could. But she didn't cross my dad often." He threw off the distant look hovering in his eyes. "So what's your most outstanding childhood memory?"

"Work," she said without hesitation.

"Work?"

Chantal nodded. "My dad ran out on us when I was eight. Cade was thirteen, Monique was eleven, and Mama was sick with a congenital heart condition."

"Monique is your sister?" he asked, surprised.

Chantal propped her elbow on the table and rested her chin in her palm. "Yeah. She and her family live in Houma."

"I didn't know you had a sister. I've heard you mention her, but I thought she was a friend."

Her smile held the same sorrow as her voice. She gave her attention to invisible hieroglyphics she was drawing on the tabletop with a short, no-nonsense fingernail. "It's funny, you know? You and I . . . we made a baby together, and we know so little about each other."

"Maybe we thought we knew everything we needed to."

The comment brought her eyes to his. "I'm not sure we ever know everything we need to."

A heavy silence filled the room. When it and the intensity in Dylan's eyes reached unbearable, Chantal resorted to her childhood tale again.

"So when Daddy left, we all had to go to work."

"What kind of work can an eight-year-old do?"

"Ironing. Weeding gardens. Picking vegetables. *That's* what I remember the most from my childhood." She shook her head as if to rid it of the unwelcome memories. "Can we change the subject? I really don't want to talk about it."

"Sure."

"It's amazing what parents do to kids, isn't it?" she said after a moment, unaware of the wistful note in her voice.

"Frightening."

"I want to be there for my baby," she said, her eyes filled with earnest desire. "And I don't want to make the mistakes your parents or mine made."

"You won't," Dylan said, his voice filled with conviction. "You'll make different ones."

The truth of what he said was prophetic, profound. No doubt he was right. She felt like bursting into tears, but knew that would do neither of them any good. Instead, she blinked the moisture away. "So what about you?" she asked.

"What about me?"

"Do you have siblings?"

"Two brothers and three sisters, but we aren't very close."

"Wow," she quipped. "Do you want a big family?"

"I think two will be enough for me."

"Me, too." But even as she said it, Chantal wondered if he was including their baby in his count.

The next day, when Gracie came to visit, Dylan had no qualms about asking her to stay with Chantal while he got out for a couple of hours. He needed to get away and try to put things into perspective. Unable to find the brass to bluff his way into her bed the night before, he'd made up the sofa. When he couldn't sleep there, he'd moved to the recliner, where he finally fell into an uncomfortable rest. It must have been around three when Chantal shook him awake and told him gently that he was welcome to share the other half of her bed. He'd taken her up on the offer, gladly. It was only when morning dawned that he realized that neither of them had done much sleeping after he joined her in her sweet-smelling bed.

There was little doubt that she was drawing him into her web again. The more time he spent with her, the stronger the pull. He needed some time to himself, needed to think about the possible ramifications of his troubling feelings, needed time to consider whether or not his presence was bothering her.

What you need is to concentrate on finding your son and forget how tempting Chantal's long legs are. What he needed to do was forget how his heart had throbbed with pain when she'd told him her strongest childhood memory.

Armed with the determination of a new day and with the composite drawing in hand, he went back to the hospital and proceeded to check with everyone on the hospital staff. It was a different shift than he'd talked to before, and he didn't care a tinker's damn if Rousseau's bunch had already questioned them. Maybe someone would remember something. Maybe he was a better interrogator.

Wanting to get it over with, he did the maternity wing first, even though he dreaded seeing that negative shake of the head from those who'd been the closest to his baby.

"No, I'm sorry," one of the nursery workers said, handing the picture back to him.

He felt his enthusiasm slip another notch, felt his heart take the added burden of another "no." He handed the composite drawing to the other LPN, who regarded it intently.

"She really looks familiar, but I can't say for certain that I've seen her in the hospital. Maybe we shop at the same grocery store. I'm sorry."

Dylan scrubbed a weary hand down his cheek and tried to smile. It was a miserable failure, even for him. He took the picture, folded it and put it in his shirt pocket. "That's okay. I appreciate your help."

The nurse nodded, and started back down to the nursery door. Dylan put his hands on his narrow, jeans-clad hips, drew in a deep breath and dropped his head to stare at the shiny tiles of the floor. What next? Talk to more nurses, hear more "no's"? Damn! When were they going to get a break?

"Mr. Garvey?"

Startled from his tortured thoughts, Dylan turned to see the LPN standing behind him. She was nervous, and there was a look of pity in her eyes that cut at Dylan's heart. Was he reduced to this, then? Pity from strangers?

"Did you remember something?" he asked, eagerness and hope vying for the upper hand.

"No, but—" She paused as if she were uncertain how to proceed. She thrust a small rectangle at him. "I thought you might like to have this."

Dylan looked down at the shiny black-and-white surface and came face-to-face with his past, his present, his future. It was a photo of a baby. His heart lurched, seemed to stop for agonizing seconds, then began to pound out a painful, measured cadence.

"It's your baby," she said, but somehow he already knew that. "We always take a picture of the newborns for the paper."

He looked up into the nurse's troubled eyes. "Thank you," he said. "I've never—" he swallowed "—seen him."

"I know. I hope it doesn't upset you—"

"No!" Dylan hastened to assure her. "I'm glad you gave this to me. I just..." His voice trailed away and he blew out a sigh. "This is pretty heavy stuff, you know?"

The LPN nodded. "I've got to get back."

"Oh, sure," he said, his mind still reeling. He grabbed her hand and pumped it up and down. "Hey, thanks, thanks a lot."

Smiling, the nurse turned and left him alone. Moving slowly, almost as if he were sleepwalking, Dylan traversed the wide hallway. He needed to go somewhere and absorb this. He passed the nursery window, whose curtains were closed. A small sign posted in the corner proclaimed that they would be open from one in the afternoon until two and again from seven until eight.

In his rental car, he turned on the engine to start the air-conditioning and took the picture of the baby from his shirt pocket. As he gazed hungrily at the tiny features and the mop of dark hair a burst of love so strong it was frightening exploded inside him. This was his baby. His flesh. His blood. His and Chantal's.

He thought of the night and day they'd made love and found it incomprehensible that what happened between them had resulted in this...a miracle. He tried to imagine the baby growing inside Chantal, changing from an act of love into a human being as it took its nourishment from her, and her body protected it from harm. That, too, was a miracle beyond belief.

Dylan searched the picture, looking for a resemblance to either him or Chantal and finding none he could pinpoint. He was unaware of the sappy smile on his face or the glimmer of tears in his eyes. His baby. This was his baby, and he wanted him back. Having a face to put with the crime upped his stake in the whole affair. Though he'd always known it was a serious matter, seeing a picture of the baby made his loss an excruciating reality.

Primed with renewed determination, he got a roll of quarters and went to a phone booth. He intended to call every psychologist and family counselor again, just to remind them how important the case was and leave Chantal's number on the off chance that one of them might have a change of heart about talking to him. If not, he'd tell the receptionists that if the doctors thought of something important, to please get in touch with Detective Rousseau.

An hour later, he'd finished. He'd done all he could.
He'd gotten no encouragement, but he felt better
knowing he'd tried. Back inside the car, he took the
picture of the baby from the dashboard. He wanted to
see him, to hold him, to tell him that no matter what
happened between his parents they both loved him . . .
would always love him.

On a sudden impulse, Dylan looked at the watch
strapped around his brawny wrist. Almost one. If he
hurried, he could make it to the hospital in time to
have a front-row view when they drew the curtain at
the nursery.

Dylan couldn't believe they were so *small*. He'd
caught fish bigger than most of the babies sleeping in
their sterile cribs. He looked at each one in turn, as if
studying them might give him some sort of insight into
his own child. The first to catch his eye was a little girl
who weighed just over five pounds. Lord, she was a
gorgeous thing, with a head full of copper-colored hair
and the prettiest little bow-shaped mouth, but she was
so tiny and fragile-looking he'd be scared to death to
hold her.

It was hard to imagine that his baby—his son—
weighed almost four pounds more. Surely he wouldn't
be afraid of a baby who was nearly twice the size of
this one. Dylan moved down the line, peering over the
shoulders of loving family members who'd come to
pay the proper homage, searching for a baby whose
birth weight was near his son's.

The closest he could find was eight pounds, fourteen ounces. Everyone kept commenting on what a big
girl she was, but, like the five-pound baby, this one

looked small to him. When she began to cry for no apparent reason, the nurse who'd given him the snapshot of his baby was there almost immediately, checking her diaper, giving her her pacifier, rubbing her back with gentle fingers.

It occurred to Dylan with sudden staggering insight that the newborns were not only small; they were helpless. Never being around babies as an adult, he hadn't realized how time-consuming just fulfilling their most basic needs must be. They were dependent on others for everything except the air they breathed. He'd never realized before what an awesome responsibility being a parent was.

Sudden nausea churned in Dylan's stomach and a shiver of fear trickled down his spine. It was unthinkable that some parents abused their role...unthinkable that some adults abused these precious innocents. He had always been sickened by the accounts of child abduction and abuse he'd come into contact with during his years as a policeman, but having a child of his own brought the horrors home in a way nothing else could.

Unable to look any longer, he turned away and headed for the exit. He tried to comfort himself with the knowledge that most people who stole babies did it because they loved children and wanted one of their own, but he was a cop and cops had long memories. The operative word was "most."

He started back to the apartment, the picture warm against his heart. Should he show it to Chantal, or would it make things worse for her? He knew she could lose control at any moment, and he didn't think he could take that. He had to present a solid front, a positive attitude.

While Dylan was gone, Chantal was joined by Gracie, who did the crossword puzzle and smoked one cigarette after the other. Then Shiloh and Micah showed up for lunch bearing wet kisses and deli sandwiches. The sandwiches were delicious; the kisses were unbearable. Though Chantal couldn't hold the wriggling baby, he was only too glad to show off by giving her kisses. Normally, she would have loved having her chin clamped down on with Micah's new teeth, but just now the unconditional love of her nephew brought a poignant ache inside her.

When Micah got cranky, Shiloh picked him up and held him close, rocking him back and forth and clicking her fingernails together in his ear.

"What are you doing?" Chantal asked.

Shiloh grinned. "Do you mean you grew up in south Louisiana and you've never seen this old Cajun trick to get a baby to sleep?"

"Never," Chantal said with a disbelieving shake of her head.

"Well, just watch."

Sure enough, in a matter of seconds, Micah had stopped his wriggling and was lying against his mother's breast, listening intently to the soft clicking noise. In another couple of minutes, his eyelids were at half mast. He was such an angel, Chantal thought, gazing at him with love and envy and sorrow.

"I shouldn't have brought him."

Chantal's startled gaze jumped to her sister-in-law's. "Of course you should have. You know I adore

Micah. It's just that seeing him reminds me of what I've lost."

"Believe me, I know." Seeing the query in Chantal's eyes, she continued, "You remember how down I was when I lost my first baby, don't you?"

Chantal remembered too well. Shiloh had lost her first child three months into what turned out to be a tubal pregnancy. She had gone into a depression that worried everyone.

"I'd been home from the hospital exactly ten days when Molly went into labor."

Though Chantal didn't know Shiloh's brother's wife well, she'd met Molly Rambler on several occasions, and liked her very much.

"My mother was staying with me, and she and Cade went to Rambler's Rest to get Laura Leigh so Garrett could take Molly to the hospital. I didn't want Laura at the house because I knew she'd remind me of what I'd lost." Shiloh gave Chantal a gentle smile. "I was right. Having her there was hard, but she was so sweet, so loving, that she charmed her way straight into my heart. I think that's when I began to see that maybe there was hope for another child."

Chantal's eyes filled with tears.

"Oh, darn!" Shiloh said. "I didn't mean to upset you I just . . ." Her voice trailed off in contrition.

"I know what you meant, and I know you're right," Chantal said in a tear-thickened voice. "And I appreciate your sharing your story with me. Really."

Shiloh laid Micah on the quilt she'd spread on the floor and went to kneel by Chantal's chair. She took Chantal's hands in hers. "Dylan will find your baby.

He's the kind of person who gets his teeth into something and won't let go.''

Chantal squeezed Shiloh's hands and gave her a wan smile. "Sort of like Micah, huh?"

"Exactly like Micah," Shiloh said with a warm chuckle. "You know, Chantal, I like your Dylan Garvey."

"You do?"

Shiloh nodded. "So does Cade. He seems like a decent sort, and I know all this is affecting him deeply."

"That's what Gracie said. You don't think he's too... hard?"

"I think being hard comes with the territory when you're in law enforcement, otherwise more cops would go over the edge than already do. But I think that way down inside Dylan is a man who needs some love and caring in his life. And I think if he got that, he'd soon learn to give it back."

Chantal thought about Shiloh's prediction long after she and the baby had gone. Should she trust her instincts? And just what did her instincts say about Dylan, anyway?

He was attractive, but he didn't seem stuck on himself the way a lot of good-looking men were. He *was* hard, but everyone agreed with that. What emotions did he evoke in her?

Trust.

Trust? Didn't he lie to you? She'd thought so, but when the facts were in, he'd been loyal to his job. He hadn't betrayed the trust of his superiors.

He made her feel safe. As if nothing could touch her. And the times they'd made love she'd known she had his undivided attention. He was totally absorbed in her and what was happening between them. She'd felt cherished . . . loved. Far more than she'd ever felt with Jeremy.

Jeremy had had a way of making her feel as though he was taking time out from his busy schedule to be with her, and that included when they made love, too. Of course, what she'd later learned was that he was actually taking time away from his lover.

"Yoo-hoo! Anybody home?" Gracie called from the back door, effectively halting Chantal's thoughts.

"In here, Gracie! Where else would I be?"

The landlady strode through the apartment, a pie held aloft. "I brought us an afternoon snack."

"If you don't stop bringing me snacks I'm going to be as big as a house. The object is to *lose* weight after you have a baby."

"You'll lose weight as soon as you start chasin' after the little critter," the landlady told her, taking the coffee from the cabinet.

The smile faded from Chantal's face.

"Now don't go gettin' long-faced on me," Gracie said, filling the carafe with cold water. "You will get your baby back."

"How can you be so sure?" Chantal said, rising and making her way through the small dining room to the kitchen.

Gracie turned on the coffeepot and took Chantal's shoulders in her bony grasp. Her gaze was steady, confident. "Because I don't think God would be cruel enough to deny you two babies. Besides, He knows you and Dylan need that child as much as you need each other."

Surprised, Chantal asked, "What are you talking about? I hardly know the man."

"You slept with him. You must have known enough," she observed, the comment so close to what Dylan had said that it was uncanny. "I've known you a long time, honey. You don't give your body or your heart lightly." She smiled and pulled out a kitchen chair. "Come on. Why don't you sit yourself down and tell me about you and Dylan Garvey."

"I've told you about him."

"I mean, tell me how you met him. Tell me how you reacted to him from the first. And tell me why you picked him to sleep with out of all the men you've had the opportunity to sleep with this past year."

"Why?"

"So you can start putting whatever it is you feel for him in perspective with what you've been through in the past and figure out what you want to do about it."

"What I want to do about it?"

"Whatever time he got away from his job is running out. He can't stay here forever. How do you feel about that? And what happens when he brings your baby home? Do you send Dylan back to New Jersey, mission accomplished—or do you try to work things out and see if you can make a real home for the child, one like you never had?"

"Make a home with Dylan?" Chantal said. "I'd never considered that."

"Never?" Gracie prodded.

"Well, it may have crossed my mind," Chantal admitted, "but not in a serious way."

"Why not?"

The pointed questions caught Chantal off guard. "Because we're so different, I guess."

"Bull. I keep telling you that you *are* alike. You're so much alike, it's scary."

The conviction in Gracie's voice surprised Chantal. "How can you say that?"

"Because it's the truth. You're both bleeding inside. I don't know what happened to cause his hurt, but regardless of what it was, it's high time you both forgot the past and got on with living. Now, stop arguing with me and tell me how you really feel about the man."

Chantal shrugged. "Okay. You want the truth. Dylan Garvey excites me more than any man I've met in a long time—maybe ever."

"Oooh...that's good."

Ignoring Gracie's lascivious grin, Chantal continued. "In spite of the fact that he scares me sometimes when he gets mad, something about him makes me feel safe." She threw up her hands in an I-don't-know gesture. "Maybe all that tough-guy macho stuff appeals to me on some deeper level."

"Let me tell you something, honey," Gracie said, leaning forward and resting her forearm on the table. "It appeals to any red-blooded woman under ninety. Why, just watchin' him walk across the floor in those tight jeans is enough to turn any woman on."

"Gracie!" Chantal cried, scandalized.

Gracie cackled and went into another of her coughing spells. "Look," she said when she'd gained control of the spasm and was drying her eyes on a paper towel, "I may be gettin' old, but I ain't dead yet."

"If you'd throw away those darned cigarettes you'd probably outlive us all."

"Probably would, but they're my only vice. I can't find a man who can keep up with me. They don't make 'em like they used to. Oh, there's a few real men still around, but they're few and far between, I'm here to tell you." She gave Chantal another wicked smile. "'Course, your brother and Dylan might be the exception. Them and that Garrett Rambler. Now *there's* a hunk if ever I saw one!"

Despite the landlady's testimonial to Dylan, Cade and Garrett, Chantal sensed a note in Gracie's voice that closely resembled sorrow. "What is it, Gracie?"

Gracie blew a stream of blue smoke toward the ceiling. "I was just thinkin' about my ex-husband."

"You were married?" Chantal asked, surprised.

"Of course I was married!" Gracie snapped. "Twice."

"What happened?"

The landlady crushed out the cigarette with an angry gesture. "*I* happened."

"I don't understand."

"I didn't, either, for a long time. That's why I'm trying to get you to see the light before it's too late."

"You aren't making sense," Chantal said. "Start at the beginning."

The veil of memory fell over Gracie's eyes. "I met him—Bill—just before the war. It was one of those quick things. Sorta like you and Dylan. We met at a USO dance, fell in love and were married ten days later. He was getting shipped out—going to Burma. I was being sent to England. He wanted to see about getting my orders changed so I wouldn't have to go. I insisted that what I was doing for the war effort was as important as what he did. We quarreled. He left. He was killed in action."

Chantal put a comforting hand on Gracie's. "Oh, Gracie, I'm sorry," she said in a broken voice.

"So am I, honey," Gracie said, clinging to Chantal's fingers.

"What about your second husband?"

"Oh, it was more of the same. He was a lot like your Dylan, and I was an awful lot like you. I wouldn't give an inch, had to have my own way and generally made things hell for both of us. Now I can see that I was scared of how he made me feel, scared if I loved him too much and something happened to him, I'd get hurt all over again. So I never let him know how much I cared. On some subliminal level, I set out to destroy us before we had a chance to make a go of it. We lived together for a couple of years, but one day he allowed that he'd had a bellyful of marriage to me, packed his bags and left."

Her smile was tinged with the sadness of forty-odd years. "And you know what, honey? I was a lot more miserable without him than I ever could have been with him, even if he'd hurt me every day of the year."

Chantal searched Gracie's lined face. "Why do I get the feeling you're trying to tell me something?"

"Because I am. Don't let what your daddy or Jeremy did to you ruin the rest of your life. Happiness doesn't just happen. You have to work at it. You have to save up the memories of the good times so that when things get bad, you can take them out and look at them and know that if you work at it, you can have good times again. If there are two things I've learned in sixty-seven years it's that pride makes a lonely bed partner, and the love of a good man can fix an awful lot of hurts.''

"But I don't know if what I feel for Dylan is love.''

"Do you think it might be?''

Chantal's gaze was steady, unwavering. "If we don't find the baby, I don't think we stand a chance. But if we do, and we had the opportunity to start over, to get to know each other—maybe.''

"Then I suggest that you pray to God that you find that baby of yours. And then I suggest that you and Dylan give yourselves whatever chance you need to try and work things out.''

Chapter Nine

As Dylan drove to Chantal's apartment, his mind was still seething with everything that had happened to him the past few days. His whole world had been turned upside down with one phone call. His future was forever changed, and all because of a few hours spent in Chantal's arms. A few hours that had resulted in a tiny scrap of humanity that shared his genes.

Dylan's emotions had taken a beating. The blinders had been yanked off, and he was being forced to deal with a plethora of emotions, the most disturbing of which was the certainty that Carole had been well within her rights to expect more from him and their marriage than he knew how to give.

Since coming to Louisiana, he was beginning to realize that a relationship, any kind of relationship, was a two-way street. How well that relationship worked depended on how well the people involved did their part. With Carole, he'd had no idea of what marriage was all about. He'd seen their marriage as being a haven to come home to after work. He would have someone there, so he wouldn't have to come in to an empty house—something he'd seldom had to do as a child and something he still hated. He'd seen Carole as a pretty, pleasant woman he could be proud to claim as his wife, someone who could satisfy his sexual needs and give him the child he wanted.

If he hadn't learned anything else from their marriage, he'd learned that his expectations were selfish, that marriage was far more than a means to satisfy his wants and needs. There was another person's wants and needs to be met, and Carole had made it clear that he'd done a poor job. In many ways he had been just what she claimed—cold, uncommunicative. But his real sin was not being what she claimed; it was running from the problem and not trying to correct his faults.

Losing Chantal because she thought he'd lied to her had pointed out that people should do more than talk; they should listen. In many ways, Chantal was like him—quick to find fault, slow to admit her own shortcomings. Like him, she was loathe to talk about the past, which was what they most needed to do. If he was a victim of parental ineptitude, Chantal was a victim of parental desertion. Yet, looking at his own childhood, he was beginning to feel that desertion was as much a mental state as a physical one.

Lord, he thought, what was happening to him? He was waxing philosophical. No. He was just coming to a full awareness that his role in his son's life was a major one, one he couldn't afford to mess up. If he was going to be the kind of father he'd dreamed of being, then his son would grow up with healthy self-esteem. If he elected not to be a part of his child's life, or if Chantal refused to let him, that, too, would have a profound effect on how the child perceived himself and his parents. The seriousness of the situation was frightening. Overwhelming. How did anyone get it right?

He imagined that successful parenting happened by pure luck—or the grace of God. He didn't know how he would manage it, he only knew he wanted to try. No more placing blame. No more running. He faced the worst of the criminal element every day in his job, surely he could face his own faults.

When Dylan arrived at the apartment Chantal had the table set for the evening meal. Pork chops were warming in the oven and the vegetables were ready to be served. A partially eaten chocolate pie sat on the stove.

Chantal had drawn her hair back into another ponytail. She was wearing loose-fitting white shorts, a hot-pink T-shirt and a hesitant smile. "Hi."

"Hi."

"Any luck?"

"No." Dylan's gaze traveled the length of her legs. "What's this?" he asked, waving a hand toward the table.

"Dinner."

"I can see that. You should have waited for me to fix something."

The sharpness of his tone didn't seem to faze Chantal. "I didn't cook this. Monique brought it by."

"Oh." He had the grace to look embarrassed. "I'm sorry I snapped. I just don't want you doing anything to hurt yourself."

From the look in her eyes, it was a toss-up as to whom the apology surprised the most. "I promise I won't do anything but sit around and get fat until I have the doctor's permission."

"Fat? Hardly. I think you're looking very well for a woman who gave birth less than a week ago," he said, ladling some purple hull peas into a serving bowl to keep from looking at her.

No doubt the unexpected compliment shocked her as much as his apology. As he set the peas in front of her, she searched his face. She was probably wondering what was the matter with him.

"Thanks. I wish I could say the same for you."

"What?" He set down a bowl of mashed potatoes.

"You look terrible."

One corner of his mouth hiked up in a wry smile. "Flattery will get you nowhere with me, lady." He turned, took a pot holder from the drawer and removed the pork chops and gravy from the oven.

Chantal refused to be distracted by his rare foray into humor. "I know it must be discouraging to go out there talking to strangers, looking for something when you don't have any idea of what that something is."

Dylan filled the glasses with ice tea and sat down across from her. He rested his elbows on the top, laced his fingers together and rubbed his mouth against the peak of his index fingers in a gesture of distraction.

"Yeah, it is," he confessed. "This is worse, though, because I have such a personal stake in it." He shook off his mood and passed her the potatoes.

Hardly aware of what she was doing, she spooned out a helping. "I'm sorry," she choked out. "If I'd let you know, none of this would have happened."

"We don't know that, so stop punishing yourself. We can't change the past," he said in his newfound wisdom. "All we can do is what's within our power to do now. Placing blame just muddles the issue."

"But if I'd told you, you might have been here and—"

The bowl of peas he'd held thudded to the table-top. "What? Stopped it from happening? Not likely. That woman picked our baby at random. She could have chosen another day, another week, another baby. The fact that she got ours was just a freak deal."

They finished filling their plates in silence. "I appreciate all you're doing," she said at last. "I wish you could have—seen him. He was so adorable. So... perfect."

Touched by the awe and love he heard in her voice, Dylan laid down his fork. Indecision warred with his need to alleviate her pain. Finally, he reached into the pocket of his sports shirt and pulled out the photo the LPN had given him.

With her forehead furrowed in a frown, Chantal took the proffered photo. A sharp gasp of recognition escaped her lips. She lifted eyes to Dylan's; a single tear slid down her cheek. "Where did you get this?"

"One of the nurses gave it to me. She thought I might want it." His throat worked as he swallowed back his own emotion. "I wasn't sure if I should show it to you or not."

For long moments, she just stared at the picture. "I'm glad you did," she said at last. "I'll put it in his baby book."

"There's something I've been wanting to ask you," Dylan said, his hesitance obvious. "But I was afraid that talking about the baby any more than was absolutely necessary might be upsetting to you."

"I don't mind talking about him," she said. "It hurts, but I think it might be healthy. I don't suppose we can ignore it forever."

"No," Dylan agreed. "We can't ignore it forever. However it turns out, it isn't going to go away."

Fear flared in Chantal's eyes. "What do you mean, however it turns out? We'll find him, won't we? You don't think anything's happened to him, do you?" she asked in a rush of new concern.

"Detective Rousseau is doing everything he can," Dylan said, hoping the placebo would calm her fear. "And no, I don't think anything has happened to him."

Chantal pushed her plate aside, virtually untouched. "You're a policeman, Dylan. You know about these things. What kind of person would take someone else's baby?"

A sick person.

But Dylan couldn't say what he was thinking. If Chantal thought the woman was disturbed, she might go over the edge herself. "Perhaps it's someone who's lost a baby of their own. Or someone who can't have one."

Or someone who wanted a baby for all sorts of grim things that were too horrible for Dylan to put into thought much less words.

"So if this woman wants a baby so badly she'll steal one, she'll be good to him, won't she? She won't hurt him?"

"No," Dylan said, telling her what she wanted to hear. "She won't hurt him."

Chantal's relief was palpable. Dylan only wished he believed himself. Deep down inside, he didn't *think* she would hurt him, but as a cop, he'd seen firsthand what the crazies had done to the world's innocents.

"What was it you wanted to ask me?" she queried, her concern allayed for the moment.

"His name. You've never told me what you named him."

Embarrassment crossed Chantal's features. "Actually, I hadn't gotten around to that yet. I wanted to name him after you, but I didn't know your full name."

If Dylan had surprised Chantal by offering her a compliment and an apology, she had just turned the tables on him. "Why would you want to name him after me?"

The question appeared to surprise her. "You're his father. It seemed right, somehow."

For long seconds, Dylan looked down at his hands that were clasped on the table. Her offer pleased him more than she would ever know. Why would she want to name the baby after him, when she hadn't wanted him even to know of their child's existence, when she was so certain they had no future together that she'd left him without a backward glance? Was it a way to assuage her guilt or to make it up to him for keeping the baby a secret?

Another, less likely reason, crept into his mind. Was it possible that the nine months of her pregnancy had caused her to realize that her feelings for him were stronger than she'd first thought? No way, he told himself, backing off that idea in a hurry. He wasn't afraid to burst into a room full of guns trained on him, but he was scared to death to even consider the possibility that Chantal might care for him. It didn't take a rocket scientist to realize that his fear stemmed from the probability that his supposition could be wrong.

"What is your full name?" she asked, rescuing him from his taunting thoughts.

Dylan wasn't aware that his eyes were filled with old griefs and lingering fears. "It's Dylan Patrick after my father, but I don't want my son named after him."

When Dylan made no move to explain, she asked, "Do you want to talk about it?"

"Not particularly," he said, "but maybe, like you said, it would help if I did." He didn't bother asking himself why he chose this person to spill his guts to. He just knew that telling her was right and fitting, just as he knew that now was the right time.

He carried their untouched plates to the sink and sat back down at the table. "My old man was a cop. Garveys have been in law enforcement since the beginning of time," he told her. "Everyone said he was a good man, a good cop. I guess he loved my mother. He brought home his paycheck every week, never ran around on her that I knew of, was home with us every weekend." He stopped and released a pent-up breath.

"But?" Chantal prompted.

"But . . . I don't know."

"You don't think he was a good man?"

"I don't doubt he was a good man, maybe even a good husband. But he was a lousy father."

"In what way?"

"Oh, he played catch with us, and he went to all our football games and wrestling matches. But he was a stranger."

"Some people don't know how to express themselves," Chantal reminded him in a soft voice.

"Tell me about it," Dylan said in a voice that reeked of sarcasm. "Paddy Garvey was a hard man. He expected—no, damn it, he demanded—our very best, and if he didn't think we were giving it, he didn't hesitate using his belt. He wanted us boys to be tough, because the world is a tough place, and he wanted us to be able to survive. If we got hurt, we weren't allowed to cry in front of him, and if we did, we never heard the last of it."

"What about your mother?" Chantal asked as she tried to reconcile what he was telling her with what she knew of him as a man. "Didn't she take up for you?"

"To a degree, but never in front of him. She'd wait until we were in bed, and when she came in to give us our good-night kiss, she'd tell us that he loved us and was just doing the best he could."

Chantal offered him a gentle smile. "Shiloh says kids don't come with instruction books, that you learn about being a parent as you go along."

"I imagine that's right."

"I do know that there is a big difference in the fathers of today and our fathers' generation. I can't imagine my dad changing a diaper, but Cade helps

Shiloh with everything. He says it's because he missed out on so much with his first two kids."

Dylan took a sip of his tea and set the glass down on a paper napkin. "I guess when someone becomes a parent they either do it the way they saw it done, or, if they think that was wrong, they go the other way."

"Probably," she agreed.

"Don't get me wrong. I believe in discipline and rules and teaching kids to have respect for people and property." He shook his head in weary indecision. "I don't know. Lately, I've even begun to think that most everything my dad did would have been okay, if he'd just balanced it out with a little love . . . if he had just hugged us and told us he loved us sometimes."

"He never told you he loved you?" Chantal asked, aghast.

Dylan's gaze was direct; his eyes were bleak. His grip on the glass tightened. "When they laid him in the ground, I'd never heard the words 'I love you' pass his lips."

"That's terrible!"

"Damn right it is. And I don't intend for my son to ever have any doubts that I love him."

If there was a challenge in his eyes, Chantal chose to ignore it. Instead, she surprised him by reaching across the table, taking his hand from the glass and curling her slender fingers around his. Her touch was warm and comforting.

"No, that's one mistake you won't make. You'll make different ones," she said with a slight smile, tossing his comment from their conversation at the hospital back at him.

As he looked at her smiling face, Dylan realized that his heart felt lighter than it had since she'd left him in Atlantic City. His hand tightened on hers, and he found himself smiling back.

"All I know is that I'm gonna try not to screw him up the way my dad did me."

"What do you mean?"

He looked at her with a lift of his heavy eyebrows. "Do you mean it's escaped your notice that because of my upbringing I'm not—let's see, how did she put it?—good husband or father material?"

"She, who?"

All pretext of good humor fled. Dylan's eyes grew distant, and his thumb rubbed over the knuckles of her hand in an absentminded caress. "Carole. My ex."

"Why would she say something like that?" Chantal asked.

"Maybe because it's true."

"And you bought into that?"

His lips twisted into a smile more bitter than sweet. "Surely you've noticed that I'm hard and cold." He shrugged diffidently. "Traits I got from my old man. In the genes, so to speak. I think you even said as much, once."

He heard the flat, emotionless tone of his voice, and recognized it for what it was. Since coming to Louisiana—since meeting Chantal, really—he'd realized that he was a walking, talking farce. The cold hardness of his demeanor was really a facade he used to hide the fact that he'd die before letting anyone know how much he was hurting inside.

"That was before I got to know you," Chantal said, refusing to flinch before the challenge in his eyes.

His low laughter held no humor. "You think you know me now?"

"I'm getting to know you better every day," she said, nodding. "Every minute."

Sudden panic gripped him. It was one thing for him to realize that he wasn't the hard case Gracie claimed him to be, the tough guy he'd gone to extremes to portray; it was something else for Chantal to get too close. Being vulnerable meant being weak. Didn't he see it every day in his work? He didn't want Chantal or anyone else getting inside him. He didn't want anyone to guess his secret: that he was scared to death of trusting his heart to anyone. Scared they'd reject it and his love the way his dad had, the way Carole had.

When Chantal had left him in New Jersey, she'd been rejecting him after a fashion, and, even though his heart hadn't been one-hundred-percent involved, it had cut him to the quick.

"Your ex-wife sounds pretty selfish to me," Chantal said now, interrupting his roiling thoughts.

"Selfish?" asked, surprised.

"Yeah, selfish. Marriage is a two-way street. It's give and take. When something's wrong, one person is *there* for the other person—or should be."

"That was the problem. I wasn't there for her." Dylan couldn't explain that he didn't know what being there meant. Let Chantal think their problems stemmed from his job.

"What about you? Was she there for you?"

"What do you mean?"

"I mean that maybe she was so wrapped up in her own problems that she didn't stop to consider what you were going through. Maybe she didn't love you enough to try and help you figure out why you behaved the way you did. Did she ever talk to you about your work when you came home depressed because you'd spent the day battling the bad guys or seen so much ugliness you wanted to throw up?''

Never, Dylan thought. Not once. Carole's concern had centered on the long hours he'd spent away from her, her own loneliness.

''There are two sides to everything, Dylan. I'm just trying to make you see that what happened to your marriage wasn't only your fault. You say you weren't there for her, well, have you ever asked yourself if she was there for you?''

Shock rendered Dylan speechless. He shrugged. ''She was there when I got home. She cooked and cleaned and kept my laundry done.''

Chantal shook her head. ''But don't you see that she was doing just what your father did?''

''What are you getting at?''

''You said it yourself when you were talking about your dad. Taking care of physical needs—cooking and doing laundry and going to ball games isn't enough. It isn't being there at all.''

Dylan didn't speak for long moments. Understanding what she was getting at dawned slowly.

''Being there is what you did when you showed up at the casino after that creep held me at gunpoint,'' she explained in a soft voice. ''It's dropping everything and flying down here at a moment's notice even though you were furious with me for not telling you about the baby. And it's helping me to the bathroom, and just—'' she shrugged ''—being in the next room worrying with me.''

He stared deep into her eyes and saw that she was serious. Was it possible that the breakup of his marriage *hadn't* been all his fault? Maybe, he thought, as hope took fragile root, there was a chance he could change.

"So," she said brightly, giving his hand a squeeze and switching the conversation to a lighter topic, "what are we going to name our baby? I'd been considering Dylan Brady. What do you think?"

"Dylan Brady." Dylan gave a considering nod. "That sounds pretty good."

The telephone rang, disrupting the first real conversation they'd shared since they'd met in New Jersey. Dylan wanted to yank the offending instrument out of the wall.

"Will you get it?" Chantal asked, disengaging her fingers from his. "I'm still not moving too fast."

"Sure." Dylan rose and went to the living room extension. "Robichaux residence."

"Mr. Garvey?" a gruff voice queried.

"Speaking."

"Detective Rousseau."

Dylan's heart sprinted forward. "Any news, Detective?"

"Not really. I just wanted to let you know that the officer I put on the hospital records has finished."

"And?"

"And there are over twenty women in the area who miscarried or lost infants at birth during the past year."

"That's a lot for a place this size."

"Most of them are low-income teen mothers who don't get proper medical care during their pregnancy."

"I see."

Dylan heard Rousseau sigh. "I wanted to let you know that we—"

"—Don't have the manpower to check them all out," Dylan finished for him.

Rousseau laughed, a tired sound that held no humor. "Ever since that composite picture came out in the paper, we've fielded dozens of calls—people who say the woman in the drawing looks like the lady down the street or claim that they saw her in McDonald's a couple of days ago. You and I both know that most of them aren't worth checking out, but we have to do it."

"I know." Dylan paused. "Look, Rousseau, what if I give you a hand?"

Rousseau laughed again. "Knowing you were going to say that, I already talked to the chief. He's pulling some kind of strings to get you a temporary jurisdiction or something."

A slow smile spread across Dylan's features. "Tell him I said thanks. I'll be in first thing in the morning to get a list of names and addresses."

"See you then," Rousseau said and hung up.

From her place in the kitchen, Chantal watched the emotions playing across Dylan's face as he spoke to the policeman. Was it only her imagination, or were his smiles becoming more frequent? One thing she was sure of—he was definitely one of the most handsome men she'd ever seen. No wonder she'd fallen for him.

Fallen for him? Was she admitting that she cared for him, then? A sigh whispered from her lips. She couldn't lie to herself any longer. What she'd told him was true. She knew him better every day, and with every day that passed, there was increasingly little doubt that what she felt for him was anything less than love. Of course, that didn't change their situation. If the cool way he treated her was any indication of his feelings, he was still blaming her for not telling him about the baby sooner.

Even though they shared the same bed—something they'd done since that first night he'd slipped into her room—never once had she awakened to find him close to her; never once had he touched her in any way. Yet despite the way he kept her at a distance, she couldn't help feeling that his presence was changing her, that he was changing, that they were growing closer in some indefinable way.

And he held your hand just now.

That was nothing. He was just accepting the sympathy she offered. Sympathy he deserved. After hearing about his childhood and his marriage, she knew for certain Shiloh and Gracie had been right. Dylan Garvey needed proof that he was loved.

For the first time since she'd learned she was pregnant, Chantal realized that their baby was as important to Dylan's happiness as he was to hers. Dylan needed the love a baby could give him, and she vowed that she wouldn't stand in the way of that. When they found the baby—they had to find him—she would gladly let Dylan share in his life.

Gracie had been right about something else, too, Chantal thought. She and Dylan were a lot alike. Both had been denied a father's love. Both had legitimate reasons for not wanting to surrender to that fickle thing called love.

Then, there was the fact that he was calling the baby "ours." She felt linked to him, as if they were bound together in a common loss, a common goal.

A soft smile claimed her lips. His surprise to learn that she wanted to name the baby after him had been genuine. When he'd asked her why, she'd found she couldn't tell him the truth: that she wanted their son named after him as a constant reminder of a night she would always remember and a man she'd never forget.

* * *

It was late afternoon, and Dylan was driving in from St. John, when the wind started to rise, dragging heavy black clouds across the sky behind it. A frowning glance toward the west convinced him that this was more than just a brief summer thunderstorm. Oh, well, he thought bitterly. At least the weather fit his current frame of mind. The expectant mood he'd awakened with had taken a turn down after he'd talked with the first five women—four of whom were really just children in women's bodies. This last one had sent his gravitating emotions plummeting like a rock tossed into the waters of the nearby bayou.

Just fourteen when she got pregnant, she had managed to keep her pregnancy a secret until her fifth month, which meant she hadn't received proper medical attention. After myriad problems, including having almost losing the baby in her sixth month, the child had been born prematurely and died soon afterward. Thankfully, Anna had made a full recovery. That was the good part. The bad part was that she looked about seven months pregnant again.

When Dylan had left the peeling house where the girl and her parents lived, his spirits were lower than they'd been in days. And now this. A stupid summer storm—and a serious one if the darkness of the sky was any indication—that would cut his day short. Maybe it was for the best, he thought with a sigh. He wasn't sure he could take too much of this in one day.

He thought about Chantal waiting at the apartment for him, her spirits buoyed by the hope that he would bring her good news. Damn! He pounded his fist on the steering wheel. Almost simultaneously, the first raindrops hit the windshield—large, fat drops that looked as if they'd been flung at him by a giant, unseen hand. More followed, and in a matter of seconds he was smack-dab in the middle of a deluge. Even though Dylan switched his headlights to bright and his windshield wipers dashed back and forth across the glass in a frenzy of motion, he was forced to slow the car's progress to a crawl.

It took him almost half an hour to drive to Chantal's through the blinding rain and gale-force winds, whose occasional hard gusts made the car shudder. By the time he pulled into the driveway, his head was pounding in sync with the deafening, staccato pulse of the rain. He sat in the car for long moments, waiting to see if the storm would abate, but even though the wind slowed, the rain continued to pelt the car.

Boredom and an increasing sense of claustrophobia sent him out into the downpour and up the steps to the porch. He was drenched to the skin by the time he'd gone three feet. Shivering from the cool rain, he hesitated before going in. If he messed up Gracie's hallway and stairs, she'd have his hide. If he stood there much longer, he'd be chilled to the bone. He wasn't sure which was worse. After a brief moment of indecision, he pulled open the door and raced up the stairs.

The apartment was as dark as the pits of hell. The blinds were closed, and there were no lights on to chase away the gloom. Sudden anxiety edged aside Dylan's surprise at finding the apartment dark and still. Where was Chantal? Had something happened?

"Chantal?" he called as he groped for the light switch near the door. He found it and flooded the living room with light.

There was no answer. Frowning, he peeled off his dripping shirt, wadded it into a soggy ball and aimed it toward the bathroom door several feet away. It landed in the middle of the floor, a shot that would have made his old high school basketball coach proud.

"Chantal?"

"In here." Her voice floated through the darkness from the bedroom.

"Are you all right?" he called, yanking off his shoes and socks and leaving them where they were.

"Yeah, I guess."

Assailed by a sudden feeling of alarm, Dylan shimmied out of his soaking jeans and sent them the way of his shirt. Then, wearing nothing but a pair of pale blue briefs, he went into the bedroom. Chantal, who was propped against both pillows, switched on the bedside lamp as he entered the room.

Dylan frowned when he saw that she was still wearing the T-shirt she'd slept in. "What's wrong?"

The fact that she wouldn't look him in the eye had nothing to do with his state of undress. "Nothing. Did you find out anything today?"

"No." Like a lone teardrop, a rivulet of water ran down his forehead past the corner of his eye and down his cheek. He brushed it away with an angry motion. The truth was, he felt like crying. His confession of defeat hurt him as much as it did her.

"It doesn't look like you've been out of bed today," he observed, hoping to divert her attention from the painfully obvious fact that he hadn't found their son.

She pushed the tangled hair from her cheek that bore a red scarlike mark caused by a wrinkle in the pillowcase. "I haven't."

Dylan recognized the symptoms for what they were, depression. His alarm factor rose another notch; his own flagging spirits took another sharp nosedive. "Why not?"

"Why should I?" she countered. "It's been six days since that woman took my baby. I'm smart enough to know that every day we don't find him diminishes our chances that we will."

She was right. Dylan knew the statistics. The chance of getting back any child missing more than seven days was a slim three percent. "I checked with six of those women today," he said, a puny offering in his own defense. "I could have done more if the storm hadn't come up."

"Oh, Dylan!" His name was a soft, anguish-laden cry. "I'm not blaming you. It's just that it all seems so useless."

When Dylan rounded the foot of the bed and sat down on the mattress next to her, she turned her face away. Gripping her chin, he forced her gaze to his. Tears of sorrow, of futility—maybe even of anger— filled her light brown eyes, trembled on her dark lashes and slipped down her cheeks in a silence that shredded his heart into hundreds of bleeding pieces.

"Damn it, don't you dare give up! Do you hear me?" The words were grated through clenched teeth. His eyes sheened with moisture, hinting of emotions he dared not unleash if he hoped to hold this whole fragile situation together.

Chantal nodded, and her hand crept up to his cheek in a gesture designed to comfort. Dylan's short, thick eyelashes drifted shut for a moment, and he drew in a deep, shuddering sigh. He couldn't let her down. He wouldn't. When he opened his eyes, they held determination.

He released his hold on her. "I'm going to go fix us something to eat, and you're going to get up and eat it, okay?"

She nodded and let her hand fall to the bed. "Okay."

Dylan rose, and, figuring it was too late to worry with false modesty, stripped off his wet briefs and pulled on clean ones he took from his suitcase. He donned a pair of running shorts and went into the kitchen to see what he could rustle up for dinner.

The cupboards looked like Old Mother Hubbard's. The fridge wasn't much better. He'd forgotten to take the pork chops out of the oven the night before and had fed them to the garbage disposal that morning. Gracie's casserole had a hard crust because he'd forgotten to put a covering over it. The vegetable crisper yielded a head of lettuce liquifying in a clear plastic bag, some mushrooms that were growing in a bed of their own fungi, and two limp carrots.

Thunder rolled and so did his stomach; he hadn't taken time out for lunch. The meat drawer held a partial package of turkey "bacon" and some low-calorie, low-fat bologna. Mmm...yummy, Dylan thought sarcastically, craving some good old-fashioned meat and potatoes.

He slammed the refrigerator door and made another survey of the cabinets, taking down a box of macaroni and cheese and a can of pork and beans. He knew from his many days as a hungry bachelor that they made a passable combination. There was a partial loaf of forty-calorie-a-slice bread in the wooden bread box that would be just dandy with the low-fat bologna.

He put the water on for the macaroni, and, on impulse, he opened the bottle of Chablis he saw found lying on its side in the cabinet. The frugal gourmet had nothing on him. Besides, he could use a glass of wine—or two—to ease the tension gripping the back of his neck. It just might help in the digestion of this meal, too.

He had assembled the sandwiches, dished up the beans and was peppering the macaroni when the lights flickered and went out. He swore. What else could go wrong? he wondered, setting the meal on the table. Though it wasn't fully dark outside, it was gloomy enough to need some sort of artificial lighting.

"Hey, Chantal! Got any candles?"

"In the drawer to the right of the sink," she yelled back.

Dylan rummaged around until he found the candles, two of the fat kind that didn't need a holder. Thankfully, he also found a box of matches. In a few seconds, candlelight spilled over the small table's dinner offering.

For a day that started out with such promise, it had certainly turned into a bummer, he thought. And so far, the evening wasn't off to a very auspicious beginning, either. As down as he felt, as tempting as it was to just throw in the towel and hop a plane back to New Jersey, Dylan knew he couldn't. There was more at stake here than his own feelings. It was up to him to get Chantal through this.

When the lights went out, Chantal's first impulse had been to scream. Fortunately, the last several days had shown her the futility of expending energy on fruitless behavior. She was worried about Dylan. Like her, he'd been excited about finally getting permission to work on the case. But something had happened to him out there today that had robbed him of the spring in his step and taken the gleam of challenge from his dark eyes. As if it wasn't bad enough that he'd had a lousy day, he'd come home and found her wallowing in her own misery. She'd like to indulge herself for the rest of the miserable evening, but she couldn't. Dylan was in there fixing her a meal—in the dark. The least she could do was act appreciative.

Sighing, she eased her feet to the floor and sat up. She found the hairbrush lying on the bedside table and dragged it through her knotted hair. Rising, she made her way through the darkened rooms. From the gleam of candlelight, she could see Dylan standing in the kitchen, staring at the table, his bare shoulders slumped in dejection. Guilt pricked her conscience.

"I see you found the candles," she said from the doorway, injecting a false cheerfulness into her voice.

Startled, Dylan turned his head toward her. "Yeah. Right where you said I would." He made a sweeping gesture toward the table. "We have gourmet delight. Sandwiches, pork and beans and the pièce de résistance, macaroni and cheese à la Garvey."

"What's that?" she asked with a smile.

"Overcooked macaroni and lots of black pepper."

He helped Chantal into her chair. Then he squared his shoulders, tossed a towel over his left forearm and raised his chin to a snooty angle. He looked ridiculous—and sexy—wearing nothing but his running shorts. "Would madam like a glass of wine with her meal?" he asked, faking a playfulness he was far from feeling.

As Chantal stared up at him in the flickering light of the candles, she was struck by a staggering feeling of déjà vu. The first night her father had walked out on them had been a night much like this one.

"Chantal? Are you all right?"

The sound of Dylan's voice brought her back from the past. "I'm fine," she said. "I was just thinking."

Dylan poured two jelly glasses half full of wine. "Not very happy thoughts from the look on your face."

"No," she agreed. "Not very happy thoughts."

"Do you want to talk about it?"

She was struck by the similarity to their conversation the night before. She knew Dylan was remembering how she'd urged him to talk about his past. It was only fair that she share hers.

"I don't mind," she said, reaching for the glass and a fortifying swallow of wine. A wistful smile toyed with her lips. "Just now, when you threw that towel over your arm and pretended to be a waiter, it was like I'd taken a big step back in time."

Dylan sat down and leaned back in his chair, his arms crossed over his chest in a patient, waiting position.

"It wasn't storming the night my father walked out on us, but the power company had shut off the electricity because he hadn't paid the bill. Mama was sick—her heart—and Monique and I were scared to death." She chuckled, a sound that held no mirth. "There weren't any groceries that night, either, and do you know what Cade fixed for dinner?"

"No," Dylan said in a soft voice, "what?"

"Box macaroni and cheese and pork and beans."

"You're kidding!"

"Cross my heart," she said, doing just that. "We were grown when he finally told us that there was no milk to put in it, so he used powdered creamer and water."

"Pretty innovative," Dylan said.

"Oh, Cade was very innovative. He had to be." She laughed again, and this time there was a trill of genuine pleasure in the sound. "You won't believe this— it's too coincidental to be believable—but do you know what he did that night they turned off our electricity and we had to eat by candlelight?"

"Don't tell me he played the waiter of a fancy French restaurant, too."

"He did!" Chantal said with another soft laugh. "Complete with a towel over his arm. Instead of it being the depressing reality it was, he turned it into an adventure. I've never forgotten that."

"You love him, don't you?"

Chantal's smile vanished. "I adore him," she said simply. "He's given us so much through the years. Things far more important than money. He worked like a dog when he was a young man, and no matter how tough things got he was always there to listen to us. Even when he got married, and later, when we did, Monique and I knew we could count on him when things got bad."

"So he was there for you when your marriage broke up?"

"Yeah." Seeing the curiosity in his eyes, Chantal said, "My husband turned out to be a real jerk. Not only did he run around on me, he did it while he claimed to be crazy about me and while I was carrying his child."

Even the dim light couldn't hide Dylan's shock. "You have another child?"

"No," she said with a sad shake of her head. "When I found out Jeremy was lying to me, we had a big fight and I left the house in the middle of a storm. I missed a turn, hit a tree and lost my baby. I was six months' pregnant."

She crossed her arms over her breasts and rubbed her upper arms as if to ward off a chill. "I think that's why I was so depressed today. The storm brought all those memories back. It was like I'd lost two babies."

The pain in her voice tugged at Dylan's heartstrings. "So you divorced him?"

"As fast as the law allowed."

Dylan mulled over her tale for long seconds. Chantal, too, was lost in thought, as old memories surfaced, bringing all their old pain. "You know," she said, her eyes contemplative, "even after all these years, whenever I see him, I want to scratch his eyes out."

"He lives around here?" Dylan asked, surprised again.

"Oh, yeah. He's the big man around town. All those Broussard Real Estate signs you see are his."

She gave herself a physical shake, as if to rid herself of the hurtful recollections. "Anyway, Cade saw me through it all."

"I can tell he's a great guy," Dylan said. "He had every reason to hate me, but I can truthfully say that he's given me the benefit of the doubt."

"Cade's fair." Her lips curved upward at the corners, but he could see the shadows of melancholy in her eyes.

"Thank God for that." Dylan gave her a quick smile and gestured to the food. "Come on, we'd better eat this wonderful meal before it gets cold."

They ate, mostly in silence, each aware that, like their shared loss, their confessions the past two evenings had drawn them closer. When Chantal finished her meal, she pushed back her plate with a sigh.

"I'm exhausted, but I don't know how I can be tired when all I do is sit all day."

"Doing nothing is what makes you tired. Boredom. Worry. If you had something to keep you busy, it wouldn't be quite so bad."

"You're probably right. Do you want me to help you clear the table?"

"Nah," he said with a shake of his head. "It won't take me but a minute to put things away. I'll just stack the dishes in the sink until morning. I doubt I'd do a very good job washing them in the dark."

Chantal rose, swaying a little as she stood. Dylan, who'd stood when she did, reached out an arm to steady her, drawing her against the hard length of him.

"You okay?" he asked, his concern obvious even in the candlelight.

Her lips curved in a weary smile. "Must be the worry and the wine."

"That'll do it every time," he told her. "Come on. Let me help you to bed."

Chantal put her arm around Dylan's lean waist and let him take her weight as they made their way to the bedroom. They were at the bedroom door when the electricity came back on. The bedside lamp illuminated her rumpled bed and the wastebasket of crumpled tissues at its side.

"Let me straighten those covers," Dylan offered, releasing her.

"Thanks. I feel so helpless."

Dylan shook the pillows and smoothed the sheets. "Make the most of it. Once we find the baby, you'll be longing for a day in bed." Before she could formulate an answer, he said, "There you go. All smoothed out."

"Thanks."

He turned to face her. "Can I get you anything before you turn in?"

"No, thanks."

"Then I guess I'll tuck you in and go do the dishes, since the lights came on."

"I haven't been tucked in since I was about ten," she told him, sitting down on the edge of the bed.

"It won't hurt you any, I promise." He helped her get the pillows placed behind her back, pulled the sheet up over her and found the paperback book she'd been trying to read. "Okay?"

"Fine, thanks."

Dylan straightened and turned toward the door. Chantal caught his wrist. "Dylan?"

His startled gaze found her troubled eyes. "Yeah?"

She tugged on his hand and he sat down on the edge of the bed. "What are you going to do tomorrow?"

"Check some more names on my list, why?"

"I want to go with you."

The pleading note in her voice tore at his heart. "I don't think that's a very good idea."

"Why not?"

"I'll be gone all day. You don't need to be out and about so soon—not for any length of time."

Her fingernails dug into his flesh; her eyes filled with tears. "You don't know what it's like, sitting in these four walls twenty-four hours a day wondering where the baby is, wondering if that woman is being good to him, knowing there isn't a damn thing I can do to change things."

"I know—"

"Damn it, you *don't* know!" she railed. She released her hold on him and clenched her fists in her lap. "At least you get out and *do* something."

In a gesture that was achingly familiar, Dylan reached out and took her face between his rough palms. With exquisite tenderness, he brushed the moisture trembling on her eyelashes. "I know this is hard for you. I know what I'm going through, and I realize that in some ways it can't compare to your grief. I didn't carry him in my body for nine months. I didn't get to see him, to—" his voice cracked "—hold him."

The pain she heard in his voice triggered more tears. She circled his wrists with her fingers, squeezing hard.

"If I don't get out of here soon, I'm going to go out of my mind."

Dylan's wide shoulders heaved with a deep indrawing of breath, and his hands pressed tighter against her cheeks. "Hang on, baby," he said, his voice rough with emotion. "Hang on just a little longer."

Drawn to the agony in his eyes, urged by the misery in her heart, Chantal swayed toward him. Dylan met her halfway, pulling her into the safe haven of his arms, holding her against his raggedly beating heart, murmuring words of comfort and encouragement into her ear while she wet his shirt with her tears.

When she drew back to look at him, the bleak agony on Dylan's face was like a rapier thrust to her heart. Blindly, wanting to assuage his pain, needing to ease her own, she found his lips with hers. The kiss wasn't one of tenderness or passion. Instead, it was filled with hopelessness, rooted in despair.

She pulled away, breathing heavily. She clutched his shirt with desperate fingers. "Find my baby, Dylan," she begged. "If you don't find my baby, I think I'll die."

Frightening emotions chased one another through the mirror of Dylan's eyes. Frustration. Desperation. Fear. He disengaged her hands from his shirt, holding her at arm's length. He released her without a word and, standing with a jerky movement, spun on his heel and left her alone with her misery.

Surprised by his sudden withdrawal, Chantal sank back against her pillows and let her tears flow. The fact that there were any tears left after the hours she'd cried throughout the day was a testimony to the mi-

raculous resiliency of the human body and the tenac-
ity of human emotions.

She heard him in the kitchen banging pans, rattling
crockery, running water in the sink. How could he go
on with the mundane things of life as if nothing was
wrong? Aching for the comfort of his arms, she cried
harder. How could he leave her when he must know
how much she ached for his touch, how much she
needed him to return the love she felt for him....

Dylan was never sure how he cleaned up the kitchen
without breaking something. All he knew was that
immersing himself in something physical had always
helped him deal with mental stress. Thunder rolled an
accompaniment to his rattling of pots and pans;
lightning blistered the sky like his curses blistered the
air in the kitchen.

What was happening to him, anyway? Nothing was
going right. His inability to learn anything about the
baby's kidnapper was playing hell with his confidence in himself, and his time in Louisiana was half
gone. To top it all off, the feelings of anger directed
toward Chantal that had carried him through the first
days of his arrival were mutating to something con-
fusing, something frightening.

Instead of that earlier resentment toward her, he
found himself overwhelmed by feelings of tenderness
and the need to protect her from any more pain. The
mere possibility that he might be falling in love with
her brought hopeless despair instead of joy. Even if
what he felt for her was changing into something more
lasting, what good would it do him? She'd made it

very clear that she wanted no part of him, and crawling wasn't in his nature or his vocabulary.

The dishes finished, he went into the living room and peeked through the French doors to the bedroom. Chantal must have cried herself to sleep. Unable to bear the thought of staying inside while his emotions were in such a turmoil, he went downstairs and out onto the porch. The night was as black as his mood. The low growling of thunder to the east indicated that the storm had passed through, but not so much as a glimmer of starlight or the brightest moonbeam penetrated the covering of thick clouds.

"I was six months' pregnant."

"If you don't find my baby, I think I'll die."

"Find my baby."

"It was like I'd lost two babies."

Chantal's confession and her heart-wrenching plea played through his mind with relentless persistence, increasing his self-imposed pressure to find their child. How could she have been so unlucky to have lost two babies? He had to find their son. Soon. Driven by a need so strong he seemed to be acting on automatic pilot, Dylan went down the steps to his rental car. He'd go by the hospital, talk to the night shift. Maybe there was someone who only worked a couple of nights a week who hadn't seen the composite picture. Maybe someone had remembered *something*.

But they hadn't. The trip to the hospital was as futile as the rest of his day had been. Sick at heart, Dylan drove along the bayou road toward Magnolia Manor. He didn't know what to do next. He didn't know what to say to Chantal that he hadn't already said. He didn't know how to ease his own heart's ache.

By the time he reached the plantation house, the westerly wind had pushed the storm clouds to the east, leaving nothing but a few wispy remnants to tickle the face of the moon, which was approaching fullness. Dylan got out of the car and began to walk along the bayou that churned and roiled in its banks like his emotions churned inside his chest.

He didn't know how long he walked; he was unaware of the soggy ground or the mud that sometimes threatened to suck the shoes off his feet. All he knew was that the farther he walked, the more at peace he felt. The moon illuminated the silent glide of an owl through the trees across the bayou and set his heart to beating with a quiet awe. The night air cooled his anger at himself, and the joyous singing of the frogs gave him a renewed sense of hope. Night birds called to one another in rituals as old as time, and the heady scents of rain-washed air and the fecund bayou soil filled his nostrils, a silent promise of a better, more fruitful, tomorrow.

He only hoped it was a promise he could count on.

Chapter Eleven

The ringing of the phone woke Dylan from a deep, dreamless sleep, the first he'd experienced in nights. He reached over Chantal and grabbed the receiver on the second ring. The scent of something softly feminine filled his nostrils. Glancing down at the classic lines of her profile, he resisted the urge to drop a kiss to her cheek.

"Hello," he said softly.

"Mr. Garvey, this is Phil Rousseau."

Hearing the detective's name wiped away Dylan's lingering sleepiness. "Can you hang on while I get the other phone?"

"Sure."

Dylan laid the receiver next to the base and went into the living room so his conversation with the policeman wouldn't wake Chantal. "What have you got?" he asked.

"Maybe nothing, but I thought it was worth passing on," Rousseau said. "One of the psychologists you contacted—without authorization, I might add," he said wryly, "called us with a piece of information she thought might be useful."

"What kind of information?" Dylan asked, his heart leaping with hope, despite the setbacks he'd encountered the previous day.

"She says that she got a call yesterday from the husband of one of her patients."

"And?"

"The psychologist—Dr. Gardener—has been seeing this guy's wife off and on over a period of six years, because she'd had several miscarriages and was determined to keep trying even though the doctors didn't hold out much hope for a successful delivery. Then, about a year ago, the patient had to have a hysterectomy. The shrink says the woman was devastated. She'd been coming in for counseling once a week until about six months ago."

"What happened then?" Dylan asked.

"No one knows, but when the husband called he told the doc that his old lady had been stuffing her clothes to simulate a pregnancy for several months."

"And he didn't try to get any help for her?" Dylan asked in surprise.

"Hey, he loves her. He didn't see any harm in it."

"So how does this tie in to our case?" Dylan asked.

"The guy called Dr. Gardener yesterday asking for advice."

"What kind of advice?"

"Whether or not he should call the police."

Dylan's head came up sharply. "Why?"

"He told the psychologist his wife had been missing for several days and wondered what he should do. He was pretty upset."

"You mean he didn't report her missing until this morning?"

"He still hasn't reported her missing. I'm getting all this secondhand. It seems the wife has pulled this kind of stunt before, so he just figured she'd show up sooner or later. Then he saw the composite drawing in the paper a couple a days ago and realized that except for the hairdo, it could be his wife."

Dylan's breath caught in his throat. Was it just a coincidence, or were they finally on to something? "Exactly how long has she been missing?" he asked.

"Since the day your baby disappeared."

Dylan swore.

"With her medical history, his knowing how badly she wants a baby and the way she's been behaving the past several months—*plus* the fact that she cut out the day your baby was kidnapped—he's convinced she's the one who nabbed your kid."

Stunned by this unexpected break, Dylan sank into the corner of the worn sofa. "Why did he wait so long to call if he's suspected her for two days?"

"He was scared, afraid we'd arrest her. He tried to figure out a way to keep her from going to jail and decided to call Dr. Gardener, who happened to remember her receptionist telling her about your call. She said she hardly slept all night for thinking about it, so she decided to give us a call just in case there might be a connection."

"There's a connection, all right," Dylan said. "I feel it in my bones."

"Me, too," Rousseau confessed. "I don't suppose you want to take a crack at this yourself?"

"I'd be delighted." Dylan wrote down the psychologist's name and phone number and said his good-byes to the police detective. Then he sat and stared at the phone for long moments, digesting the information he'd just received and filtering it through what he knew about such cases. The certainty that they were finally on to something grew.

Trying to hold the burgeoning hope at bay, Dylan gathered clean clothes and took a shower. More than ready to get started, he got the psychologist's name from the notepad by the living room phone and realized his billfold was on the nightstand.

Making as little noise as possible, he went back into the bedroom where Chantal still slept. Sweet heaven, she was gorgeous, he thought, looking down at her sleeping form. Her heavy red brown hair lay in tangled disarray against the floral sheets. Her skin glowed with returning good health. The thought of leaving her was unbearable. The urge to wake her and tell her the latest news was almost overwhelming, but recalling her agony from the night before, he knew that getting her hopes up might just lead to another disappointment if this lead turned out to be a dead end.

Unable to resist a stronger impulse, he reached out and touched her cheek with the tips of his fingers. Still asleep, she turned toward his hand, nuzzling her face against his palm like a puppy seeking affection. The fact that she had turned to him in her sleep, just as she had the night before when she'd sought comfort in his arms, was a balm to his battered soul, one of the sweetest moments of his life. Carrying the memory like a talisman, he wrote her a note explaining that he'd gone to check out a new lead. He left the apartment and headed for the psychologist's house.

Darlene Gardener lived in one of Thibodaux's most prestigious neighborhoods. While the houses there were large and grand, Dylan realized he liked Magnolia Manor better. Actually, he liked Gracie's house better. The older houses had character, something their new counterparts lacked.

He got out of the car and went to the door, trying his best to forget he had a personal stake in the upcoming meeting. He was a cop, he told himself as he pressed the doorbell. This was just another job. Making himself believe the lie was another matter.

Darlene Gardener was not what he expected. Tall, svelte, blond, she looked more like a model than a therapist. She greeted him with a smile and led the way to the living room, which was big enough to set Chantal's entire apartment in.

"I've already called Mr. Palmer and told him we'd be coming over to talk to him," she said. "Would you like a cup of coffee before we go?"

"No, thanks." Dylan was anxious to be on his way.

"Let me tell my husband goodbye and get my purse, then."

She returned in a matter of minutes, and preceded Dylan out to his car. Once she was ensconced in the passenger seat, he said, "I really appreciate your help."

"No problem. I just wish Mr. Palmer had called sooner."

"Me, too. By the way, be sure to thank your receptionist for me."

Darlene Gardener laughed. "I'll do that. She was pretty impressed with your persistence."

"Otherwise known as desperation."

The psychologist sobered. "I know this has been hard for you. How is your wife taking it?"

Dylan's jaw tightened. "Chantal and I aren't married."

"I see. In any case, how is she doing?"

"When she first found out what was going on, she was totally distraught. But I arrived last Friday morning, and until last night, she's been okay. Maybe a little too controlled. But we've been doing some serious talking, and she finally broke down and had a good cry last night. I don't know. Maybe it was a good thing."

"No doubt about it. I'm glad you were there for her."

Vincent Palmer was about Dylan's age. Unlike Dylan, he was balding and had let himself go soft.

"This is the baby's father, Vincent," Darlene said, having told Dylan they might get further if the man didn't know he was a policeman.

Dylan held out his hand; the man took it in a limp grip. "How do you do? Look," he said, stepping aside for them to enter the foyer, "I don't know what else I can tell you."

"Just tell me what you told Dr. Gardener," Dylan encouraged him as he followed the man and Darlene into the living room.

Vincent Palmer told how his wife—Gloria—had stopped seeing the doctor and how she'd stuffed her clothes to make herself look pregnant. He told how she'd flaunted her "pregnancy" to her friends and neighbors and how embarrassed he'd been.

"You knew her behavior wasn't typical, Vincent. Why didn't you call me?" Dr. Gardener asked.

His eyes filled with tears, and he looked down at the his hands as they twisted in his lap. "Because I was afraid you'd want to send her away somewhere." He glanced up. "It was embarrassing for me, but it made Gloria happy, and it seemed a harmless-enough pastime." Vincent Palmer went on to explain how his wife had failed to come home the day Dylan and Chantal's baby was taken and how she hadn't contacted him since.

"Did Gloria take any of her clothes?" Dylan asked.

"Several things, yes," Vincent said with a nod. "And she took all the baby clothes."

Dylan and Darlene exchanged a sharp glance.

"What baby clothes, Vincent?" the psychologist asked.

"The things she'd been buying for when the baby came."

"Did she say anything that might have been a clue as to what she had in mind?" Dylan asked. "What was her attitude?"

Vincent Palmer gave the questions thoughtful consideration. "Now that I think of it, she seemed excited."

"Excited?"

"Not excited, really. More like she had a secret." The distraught man rubbed his temple as if a pounding headache throbbed there. "And when I left for work, she said that she knew she had a month to go but that she didn't think she could wait any longer."

The more he talked to the man, the less doubt there was in Dylan's mind that Gloria Palmer was innocent. The thought that his baby's welfare—his very life—depended on this woman sent a shiver of apprehension through him. "Do you have a picture of your wife handy?"

"In the bedroom," he said, rising. "I'll get it."

"What do you think?" Dylan asked as Vincent left the room to get the photo. "Could she have done it?"

Darlene nodded. "From what I know about it, she's exactly the type who would do this kind of thing—hyper, very emotional, the hysterical type—and from what Vincent has told us, it sounds not only possible but very probable."

Vincent Palmer returned with an eight-by-ten glossy of his wife. He handed it to Dylan, who swallowed back a curse. Even without looking at the composite drawing Chantal had helped create, there was no doubt in his mind that he was looking at the likeness of the woman who had taken his son.

With his heart beating out a tortured rhythm, he reached into the pocket of his shirt, drew out the police drawing and unfolded it. Gloria Palmer had shoulder-length curling hair; the woman Chantal had described had short hair—probably a wig. Other than a softening of the sternness in the drawing and a slight fullness to her face that a slight weight difference might have contributed to, the two women might have been twins.

"Bingo," Dylan said, passing both pictures to the doctor.

Darlene looked at them and passed them to Vincent Palmer, who licked his dry lips. Dylan saw his narrow shoulders begin to shake. When Vincent raised his head, two tears slid down his cheeks. "I'm sorry," he said in an anguished whisper. "Dear God, I'm so sorry."

Dylan wanted to tell him it wasn't his fault, but before he could form the words, Vincent asked, "What do we do now?"

"We try to find them."

"How?"

Dylan placed the composite back into his pocket. "We look in all the obvious places first. If she isn't there, we try another approach."

Vincent nodded.

"What about her parents or a close friend?" Dylan questioned. "Would she go there?"

"Her parents are dead, and she has no close friends."

"Okay," Dylan said. "What about favorite places the two of you liked to go, or any second homes where you went to get away from things?"

Vincent frowned. "We don't have any favorite vacation spots," he said, with a slow shake of his head. "Gloria didn't like being away from home much. My parents did leave us a camp house on Lake Bistineau up in the northern part of the state, but we don't get up there very often."

"Have you checked there?

"There's no phone at the cabin."

"I'd like the address," Dylan said.

Vincent wrote the address down on a notepad, tore off the sheet and handed it to Dylan. "It's down near Camp Joy."

Dylan added that tidbit of information and pocketed the small piece of paper. "Can you think of anything else that might help us?" he asked, standing.

"Not offhand."

Dylan and Darlene shook hands with him and started for the door. "Be sure and give Dr. Gardener a call if you think of anything," Dylan said, holding the door for the doctor.

"I will."

They were halfway down the sidewalk when Vincent Palmer halted them. "What's going to happen to Gloria when you find her?"

Dylan and Darlene exchanged a troubled glance. "She's going to need a lot of help, Vincent," the doctor said. "We'll have to see that she gets it."

Satisfied with the answer, the man shut the door.

"What now?" Darlene asked as Dylan helped her into the car.

"We go to the police station and tell Rousseau what we have. We have him get the state police to check out the address Palmer gave us. If she's there, we send someone in to negotiate the baby's release. If not, we go to plan two."

"What's that?"

"Beats me," Dylan said. "In the meantime, I'm going to have Rousseau call Palmer and get her credit card numbers. We can run a check to see if she's used them the past week, and if so, we might be able to see what she bought and where she bought it. If she hasn't panicked, she might still be in the area where she made the purchases."

Dylan and Darlene spent the next couple of hours at the police station. When they got word that the camp house on Lake Bistineau showed no signs of having been inhabited in some time, Dylan's heart plummeted. He was pacing the squad room floor when Rousseau stuck his head out of his office and said, "We got something."

"What?"

"She bought some formula and baby things at a discount store in Jefferson."

"When?" Dylan asked, the blood rushing through his veins with dizzying speed.

"Last night."

"Thank God," Darlene said with a smile. "Thank God."

"She also charged some baby clothes and had them sent to a motel in Metairie."

"Give me the address," Dylan said. "I'm going to call Chantal and tell her the news, and then I'm on my way."

"Whoa," Rousseau said. "First of all, you're crazy to call her and get her hopes up. This might be a false alarm. Second, you should let someone else do this."

Dylan felt as if he'd been slapped in the face. "Why?"

"Because we're gonna treat this as a hostage situation, Garvey. You're too close to the situation. Sorta like a doctor operating on a member of his family. We don't know what this woman will do if she's cornered."

"I don't think she'd ever hurt the baby if that's what you're getting at." Darlene spoke up quickly, glancing from Rousseau to Dylan and back again.

Rousseau's gaze was implacable. "Can you promise that?"

"Of course not."

"And what about Gloria Palmer?" Rousseau queried. "Can you promise me she won't do herself in if we go in for the kid?"

"She's classic manic-depressive," the therapist said thoughtfully. "I suppose there's always the chance that she might try to harm herself."

Rousseau's firm gaze found Dylan's. "That's what I thought. So it's my way or the highway. *I'm* going."

"Not without me," Dylan said. The look in his eyes said, And I dare you to try and stop me.

"All right, since you insist," Rousseau said with exaggerated sarcasm. "We're going in an unmarked car, no sirens, no backup. I don't want to scare her. Something tells me the less fanfare the better on this one. Oh, but we are taking the doc, here, with us."

Dylan agreed with Rousseau's plan wholeheartedly. "Good idea. She can help us talk to Gloria."

"Wrong. Don't you remember any of your hostage training, Garvey? I'm not gonna let Dr. Gardener talk to her. She's goin' along to take care of the baby once we get our hands on him."

"The token female, detective?" Darlene said with a twist of her pretty lips.

"Well, I sure as hell don't know what to do with a kid."

"In that case I'll be glad to go," Darlene said. "Do you think we should call Vincent and ask him to come along?"

"Vincent?" Rousseau exploded. "The husband? You been watchin' too much TV, doc. The worst thing you can do is get a priest or a family member to talk to them."

"I don't understand."

"You oughtta know that a lot of these people who decide to off themselves want an audience. They want someone to know why they're doing it."

The psychologist looked horrified. "Look, just because I said it was a possibility, we aren't talking about a murderer or a potential suicide here. We're talking about a disturbed woman who's stolen a baby."

"Every hostage situation is a potential homicide," Dylan said, knowing Rousseau was right to follow procedure.

"Doc, you're the intelligence gatherer," Rousseau announced during the ride to Metairie. "You tell me everything you can about Gloria—what she likes, what agitates her, all that kind of stuff. The more I know about her, the better my chances are of talking her into handing over the baby and going back with us."

"Okay."

"I'm the primary negotiator, which means I'll do the talking. And Garvey," Rousseau said with a grin, "well, he's along because I'm not big enough to make him stay behind. And maybe, just maybe, I might need him."

Dylan wasn't fooled. He knew well what his role was. If—God forbid—things turned bad, he was the containment officer, which meant that when Gloria Palmer left the motel room, he'd have his thirty-eight aimed at her.

When they reached the motel, Dylan followed Rousseau into the office. Both policemen drew breaths of relief to learn that Gloria Palmer was still there. Dylan kept silent while Rousseau explained to the manager what was going on and asked to see where her room was located. They found the curtains drawn tight. There was no chance of seeing in.

Finding that there was no connecting door to her room, Rousseau asked for a phone with an extension so Dylan and Darlene could monitor his conversation. When he was sure everything was set, Rousseau had the desk clerk connect him to Gloria Palmer's room. He gave a thumbs-up sign as the phone rang.

She picked up on the fifth ring. "Hello?"

Dylan could hear the wary note in her voice and felt his gut clench in reaction. Though he didn't deal with hostage negotiations, he knew that the initial confrontation with the hostage-taker and the moment of surrender were the two most critical times. Right now, Gloria Palmer was wondering who was calling, fearing she'd been found out. When Rousseau identified himself, she'd panic, imagining guys in police windbreakers breaking down the door, their guns blazing. That was the moment she'd be most inclined to do something desperate.

"Hello, Gloria," Rousseau said in a friendly, mellow tone. What Rousseau was counting on—what any cop counted on—was that the calm voice on the other end of the line would ease the hostage-taker's fears.

"Who is this?" she shrieked. "How do you know who I am?"

"My name is Phil Rousseau. I'm with the Thibodaux police, and I'm here to help you."

"I don't need any help," she said, her voice shrill, edgy.

"Well, that's not what I was led to believe. Your husband called Dr. Gardener this morning and said you hadn't been home in several days. He's real worried about you, Gloria."

"You talked to Vincent?" Her voice echoed her surprise.

"Yes, ma'am, just a few hours ago."

For a moment, Dylan wondered why Rousseau was talking about the husband and not the baby, when he remembered that the object was to make Gloria believe that she—not the baby—was of greatest importance to them.

"We just want to take you back home."

"That's a lie," Gloria snapped. "You aren't here to take me home. You're here to get the baby."

Rousseau's gaze found Dylan's. She did have the baby! That was good news. The fact that she was ticked off about being discovered was bad. Dylan's heart began to beat out a heavy, ragged rhythm.

"I'm here to get you both, Gloria," Rousseau said truthfully, honesty being the best policy in this type of situation. "I understand you've been through a lot the last year or so."

"Did Vincent tell you that?"

"Yeah. He said you couldn't have a baby of your own. That's gotta be tough, especially when you want one so badly."

Dylan heard her sob. "You don't have any idea," she said. "Vincent wants a son. I lost six babies in five years, and then I got cancer and had to have a hysterectomy." She sobbed again.

"That happened to my wife," Rousseau said.

"You're lying!" she said in a sharp tone. "You're just trying to butter me up so I'll give you the baby."

From somewhere in the motel room, Dylan heard a sudden wail. The baby was crying. What was happening? Had Rousseau really made her mad? Was she hurting him? Dylan's heart sank. *Easy, Rousseau. Take it easy.*

"I wouldn't lie about something like that, Gloria."

If Gloria Palmer could see the bleakness in the detective's eyes she'd have no doubt about his telling the truth. A long period of quiet stretched over the phone lines; the baby's loud crying providing a background for the silence.

"Is everything okay?" Rousseau said when the waiting approached unbearable.

There was no answer from Gloria Palmer. The baby's crying hushed with alarming suddenness. Panic rose in Dylan on silent black wings. He leaped up and started for the door. Angrily, Rousseau gestured for him to stay put.

"Gloria!" he snapped. "Is everything all right?"

The soft, girlish giggle that echoed over the phone lines grated on Dylan's jangled nerves. "Of course everything's all right," Gloria Palmer said in a smug tone. "I just had to change the baby's dirty diaper."

Rousseau and Darlene exchanged relieved smiles. Dylan heard the unseen woman humming an off-key lullaby under her breath. He closed his eyes in agony. *God, please.* He wasn't a praying man, but he found himself asking—begging—for divine intervention.

"He's asleep," Gloria said at last. "Did you and your wife have children before she got sick?" she asked.

"Yeah, but they're grown now. But you know what, Gloria? If Pat had gotten sick like you back when we were having our kids, and if I'd had to decide which was most important, I'd pick her every time. I bet your husband feels the same way."

"I don't think so."

"Have you asked him?"

"Well, no."

"Don't you think it might be a good idea?"

"Is he there?" Gloria asked, anticipation lacing her voice. "Can I talk to him?"

"He isn't here," Rousseau said.

Another long silence ensued. "I don't know what all the fuss is about," Gloria said at last. There was anger in her voice. "The father doesn't care for the baby or he'd have been around for the mother. And she doesn't even have a job. I can take far better care of him than she can. You'd think she'd be grateful."

"Take it easy," Rousseau soothed. He glanced at Dylan, whose jaw tightened ominously. "I see your point, but how do you know all this?"

"I heard the baby's mother talking to her brother," Gloria said serenely.

"Well, you know how easy it is to misjudge things," Rousseau said in a placating voice, "and I can assure you that you're wrong. The baby's father wants him very much. And the mother—Chantal—is very upset. It might be hard for her, but she'll manage. Now, why don't you bring him out and let us take him back before this gets any worse?"

"What do you mean?" There was no mistaking the worry in her voice.

"I mean that if you don't give me the baby, they'll just send more cops. Then the press will get ahold of it and..." He let his voice trail away. "You know how the press is."

"Oh, my," she said. "Vincent will be furious if the newspapers get ahold of this."

"You'd know more about that than I do," Rousseau said noncommittally. "But I'm sure you don't want to upset him."

"No." There was a slight pause. "All right," she said, "I'll give you the baby."

Dylan drew a deep breath of relief. Darlene squeezed his shoulder. Rousseau didn't blink an eye.

"I think you've made a very wise choice, Gloria," he said.

Dylan got his attention and mouthed, "I'm going in for the baby."

Rousseau gave a sharp, negative shake of his head. "What I want you to do is bring the baby out to the parking lot in five minutes. I'll move my car around by your room. It's a blue Grand Am. You'll be able to see it from the window. Just bring the baby out to me, and I'll take you to see your husband."

"All right."

"Good. Look, I'm gonna hang up now and go move the car. When everything's ready, I'll have the manager give you another call. You don't even have to answer. Just bring the baby out."

"Okay."

Rousseau hung up. He looked as if he'd just run the New York City marathon.

"Thank God!" Darlene Gardener said. Grinning widely, she gave Dylan a hug.

Rousseau scrubbed a hand over his haggard face. "No dancin' in the streets until we have our hands on the baby and Mrs. Palmer in bracelets."

Dylan knew he was right, that it wasn't over until the fat lady sang, but he couldn't stop a rising elation as Rousseau called the Metairie police and asked for an unmarked car to come quickly, no sirens, no lights. Then, at Rousseau's suggestion, Dylan took a place around a corner from Gloria's room, out of view. Though it wasn't a good idea, if he had to, he'd rush her. Darlene went with Rousseau. When everyone was set, the manager called the room.

They waited. One minute. Two. The door stayed shut. Dylan's palms began to sweat. Where was she?

What was going on? Finally, the manager came barreling around the corner. He skidded to a stop a few feet from Rousseau. Dylan couldn't hear what he said, but he saw Rousseau throw up his hands in despair and follow the manager back toward the office. Dylan left his spot and caught up with them.

"What's going on?"

"She changed her mind," the Thibodaux cop said in disgust. "Happens all the time. She freakin' changed her mind."

Dylan's euphoria vanished like a rabbit in a magic trick. "What do we do now?"

"Start over." At Dylan's look of shock, he added, "Hey, all we got is time—right?"

Back inside the office, Rousseau was connected to the room again. This time, Gloria answered promptly.

"Gloria," Rousseau said, again the cool, collected cop with a world of patience. "What happened?"

"Who's that with you?" she shrilled. "Is it another policeman?"

"You mean the woman? That's Dr. Gardener. I brought her along, because I thought you might feel better on the ride back with a woman to talk to." An out and out lie. Gloria wasn't going home. She was going to the police station.

There was no response for several long minutes. "Are you going to put me in jail?" she finally asked, her voice quavering.

"That's not my department, Gloria," Rousseau evaded. "I'm just here to take you back safe and sound. But I do know that we'll get you all the help possible. Dr. Gardener—all of us—are anxious to help you get through this."

Again, Dylan realized that the cop was being as truthful as he could.

He was waiting for more arguments when Gloria said, "Okay, I'm coming out."

Dylan could tell that her sudden capitulation surprised Rousseau, too. He wiped his forehead with a wrinkled handkerchief. "Don't let me down, Gloria, okay?"

"I won't."

And she didn't. By the time Dylan and the policeman got back to their places in the parking lot, Gloria Palmer was handing the baby over to Darlene Gardener, who drew him into a close embrace. He could see the woman's shoulders shaking, and despite the pain she'd caused him and Chantal, Dylan felt his heart constrict in empathetic pain. He knew what it was like to want, to need, a child so desperately.

As he watched, two plainclothes cops approached and handcuffed Gloria Palmer. Rousseau said a few words to Darlene and met Dylan halfway to the car. "Your kid looks fine. I'm going to ride down to the station with Gloria. You and Doc take your baby home."

Dylan gripped the detective's hand. "Thanks." It was all he could think to say, and it wasn't enough.

"Tell me that when he's sixteen," Rousseau said with a weary grin.

Dylan watched the policeman get into the car with the Metairie cops. He didn't want to admit it, but his fear of going to see his son for the first time was as great as his need. He glanced at Darlene Gardener, who smiled.

"He's beautiful."

Like a man under the influence, Dylan crossed the asphalt to where she stood holding his baby. He wasn't prepared for the jolt of love that rocked him to his very soul. The baby might have been big, but he looked so small, so helpless. He was awake, squinting up at them with dark blue eyes. His tiny fists flailed the air in typical jerky infant fashion. They stilled, and, knowing his son wouldn't reject the overture, Dylan reached out and touched the softness of one miniature hand with his little finger. Instinctively, the baby's fingers closed around his.

He was lost. Captive to this tiny person who he was sure would spend the next eighteen years leading him around by the finger he now grasped. The thought of leaving him was unthinkable, but unfortunately, it didn't seem he had much choice.

"What's his name?" Darlene asked.

"Brady." Dylan spoke without hesitation. "Dylan Brady."

"That's a great name." She held the baby toward him. "Here. Would you like to hold him while I drive us back?"

Did he want to hold him? Dylan could think of nothing in this world he wanted more. "I don't know how."

"Fake it," she said with a smile.

"Okay," he agreed, "but I've got to call Chantal first."

"Go ahead," the psychologist said. "Brady and I aren't going anywhere."

Chapter Twelve

"I'm getting worried," Chantal told Gracie that afternoon as she and the landlady sat visiting and drinking coffee.

"Why's that?"

"Dylan was gone when I woke up this morning, and he hasn't been back since." Chantal's brow puckered. "It isn't like him to be gone so long."

"Did he say where he was going?" Gracie asked, popping the last bite of an old-fashioned tea cake into her mouth.

"No. All his note said was that Detective Rousseau had a new lead." Her haunted gaze focused on some point across the small room. There was unutterable weariness in her voice. "I'll be so glad when this is all settled—one way or the other."

"What do you mean, one way or the other?" Gracie asked in a testy voice.

"I'm not naive, Gracie," she said, tears pooling in her eyes. "I heard on one of the talk shows that after a week, the chances of getting a child back drop dramatically." She twisted her fingers together. "If they don't find him, I need to figure out what I'm going to do. I've got to find some kind of job and get on with my life. I've got to make plans...."

"I've been meaning to talk to you about that."

"About making plans?"

"Yes." Gracie poured another cup of coffee and lit a cigarette. "I don't want you to think this is charity—"

"I'm not taking money from you, Gracie," Chantal interrupted.

"Well, that's good, 'cause I'm not giving you any." She took a drag off her cigarette and blew the smoke ceilingward. Her smile was bittersweet. "You know I been sayin' these things are gonna kill me? Well, I was right. Doc Mason says I've got emphysema."

"Gracie!"

"Oh, I'm not checking out any time soon, but I got to thinkin' that maybe I ought to get my affairs in order. So I went to a lawyer and had this place made over to you with the stipulation that I get to live here as long as I want or until I die—whichever comes first. Truthfully, I've been thinking about moving into one of those cute little apartments across town."

"Why would you give your house to me?" Chantal asked, surprised and touched by Gracie's generosity.

"Why not? I don't have any young'ns of my own, and you're about as close as I'm likely to get. You and that man of yours can move downstairs when I'm gone and rent out the apartments, or you can fill it full of kids of your own. Heck, you can sell the place if you want. Makes no matter to me.''

Chantal felt moisture gathering in her eyes. She reached out and covered the old woman's gnarled hand with hers. ''Gracie, Gracie, what can I say?''

''No need to say anything.'' The older woman cleared her voice and stubbed out the cigarette. ''This place won't make you rich, but you'll have a roof over your head and the rent you earn will take care of your utilities and groceries.''

Chantal squeezed the landlady's blue-veined, be-ringed hand. ''You're a good friend, Gracie Metcalf, and I love you.''

Gracie snorted. ''Save that kind of talk for your Yankee.''

Chantal smiled. ''I don't think he's interested. Besides, there's enough to go around.''

Before Gracie could respond, the phone rang. She leaped to her feet. ''That's probably him now.'' She snatched the receiver off the base. ''Hello.''

''This is Dylan, Gracie. Is Chantal handy?''

Wordlessly, with a wink, Gracie handed the phone to Chantal. ''Dylan!'' she cried. ''Where are you? I've been worried sick.''

''I'm in Metairie.''

''Metairie? What are you doing there?''

''I came to get our baby,'' he told her. ''I'm bringing him home right now.''

Dylan saw Cade and Shiloh's car as soon as the car turned the corner. There was another vehicle he didn't recognize. Darlene pulled his rental car to a stop. Cradling the baby close, he said, ''I don't know what to say, except thanks, Doc.''

"My pleasure."

"Why don't you take the car to your house. I'll pick it up later."

She nodded. "If either you or Chantal need to talk, just give me a call. It'll be on the house."

"I might take you up on that," Dylan said, reaching for the handle. He got out, slammed the door and watched as she put the car in gear and pulled out onto the street.

Holding Brady in the crook of his arm, he let himself in and started up the steps. When he reached the apartment door, it swung open as if some sensor was monitoring his approach. Dylan was aware of people standing around—Cade, Shiloh, Gracie, Monique and a man and three kids he didn't recognize, probably Monique's family—but his gaze was focused on Chantal, who stood in their midst, her eyes glowing with happiness and the sheen of tears. Dylan went to her and, without a word, placed Brady in her arms.

"Thank you," she said, and burst into tears.

He wanted to draw her and his son into his arms, but he held back, and the next thing he knew she was being enfolded in Cade's embrace. Her family flocked around her like wagons drawing into a protective circle. Feeling as necessary as a bicycle to a fish, Dylan backed away a few steps. The adults were laughing and crying and joking. They oohed and aahed and nuzzled and kissed. The three children craned their necks to see and were lifted up to get a better look. He watched as they made Chantal sit down so she could undress Brady and count his fingers and toes.

Dylan could never remember wanting anything in his thirty-five years as much as he wanted to be a part of the joyous reunion taking place before him, as much as he wanted to be a part of a loving, caring, stick-by-your-side family. He rubbed at his suddenly burning eyes.

He started to turn away, but from across the room, Chantal looked up and met his gaze. There was an emotion on her face he couldn't define. For the space of a heartbeat, he thought she was going to say something, hoped she would call him over to join them, but one of the children asked her a question, and she turned to answer him with a laugh.

The tender sprout of hope growing inside Dylan withered. With the breezy chatter and euphoric laughter ringing in his ears, he escaped into Chantal's bedroom. Even with the French doors pulled shut, he could hear the sounds of their gaiety. Even with the blinds closed, he could picture their smiles.

Hardening his heart to the vicious talons of pain that tore at it, he took his suitcase from the closet and started gathering his things. He didn't know why he was so upset. Nothing had changed, he thought, throwing a shirt into the yawning suitcase. His dream, the one he'd nurtured ever since Chantal had called and told him about the baby, the one where he was a better father than his old man ever hoped to be, was just that—a dream.

As much as he might want a wife and child, as much as he might want to be part of a family like Chantal's, it wasn't in the cards. Carole was right. Being a cop wasn't conducive to maintaining a thriving relationship or raising a family. He'd witnessed too much ugliness, been a part of too much pain.

Breathing heavily, he slammed the suitcase shut and stood with his hands on his hips, his head bowed. Being shut out of his son's life might hurt now, but it would hurt a lot more later. It was best he just went back to the city and let Chantal and Brady make their own life.

Taking out the phone book, he dialed the airport to make reservations for a flight back to Atlantic City. According to the ticket agent, he was lucky. There was a seat left on a mid-morning flight the following day. With nothing left to do but get through the next eighteen hours, Dylan left the room and edged his way around the crowd in the living room. No one seemed to notice, which was just as well.

He was sitting on the porch steps watching the sun set when he heard the screen door slam shut and Cade joined him.

"That's quite a circus up there," Cade said.

"Yeah."

"I want to thank you for finding the baby and bringing him back to Chantal."

Dylan shrugged diffidently. "It was luck."

"If you ask me, persistence played a major part in finding him. You kept at those people, kept it on their minds. If you hadn't, that receptionist might not have said anything to Dr. Gardener."

Dylan didn't reply. His mind was on the woman and child upstairs.

"How much more time do you have off?" Cade asked. "I was thinking that now that everything's sort of settled down, maybe we can get in some fishing before you go."

The offer surprised as much as it pleased Dylan. He wished he'd had the opportunity to get to know Chantal's brother better. "I appreciate the offer, but I'm flying out in the morning."

"I never had you pegged as a quitter."

The casual statement brought Dylan's head up sharply. "It's hard to be a quitter when you don't even enter the fray," he said.

"Maybe I'm missing something here," Cade said, his penetrating gaze boring into Dylan's. "I thought you loved my sister."

Dylan rose in one swift movement. "Damn it, I do!" he said almost angrily. When he realized what he'd just admitted, he looked down at Cade with something close to disbelief in his eyes. His voice softened. "I do."

"Then why are you leaving without fighting for what you want?"

"Because Chantal has had too much heartache in her life already." Dylan planted his hands on his hips in a gesture of defeat. "I have it on good authority that I'm not good husband or father material. Even I'm smart enough to realize that my job makes me a bad marriage risk. I don't want to be the reason for her pain. I couldn't bear it if I was."

"If you leave her and the baby you'll be causing more pain than you'll ever know."

"Has Chantal said that?"

"No," Cade replied. "But I know my sister, and she's an awful lot like you."

Chantal was glad when everyone left. She'd enjoyed their coming, had wanted them to be there for the return of the baby, but she was tired and the baby was hungry. She just wanted to be alone with him, to cuddle and love him to her heart's content. And she imagined Dylan would want to hold him, too. Where was Dylan? she wondered as she prepared a bottle of premixed formula she'd brought home from the hospital.

Since she wasn't supposed to lift the baby, who she was already beginning to think of as Brady, she lay down on the bed next to him and offered him the bottle. He took the nipple eagerly. Chantal was glad to see his appetite was good; she was saddened to think that Gloria Palmer's actions had cost her the pleasure of nursing her son.

Shaking her head to rid herself of the unpleasant memory, she brushed a kiss to Brady's downy head. He was here; he was all right. She should be thankful for that instead of grousing about something as trivial as not getting to nurse him.

Her fingers trailed over his cheek, and she found herself wondering what Dylan thought of his son. Where was Dylan, anyway? she asked herself again. He'd certainly made himself scarce while everyone was here. She recalled the moment she'd caught his eye across the room. He'd looked as if he wanted to say something. He'd looked sad. Then Michael had asked her a question and when she'd looked for Dylan again, he was gone. Maybe he'd left because, like the greedy soul she was, she'd allowed herself and her family to monopolize the baby.

Now that things had settled down, her woman's instinct told her why Dylan was sad. It was very simple: he needed Brady as much as she did.

The realization had no more than crossed her mind when she heard his key in the lock. With her heart pounding in her chest, she waited for him to come in and wondered what they would say to each other now that the crisis was over. Though the carpet muffled his approach, she knew the moment he stepped into the bedroom.

She raised her head to look at him. He stood in the opening, one hand braced on the doorjamb. Her breath caught at his sheer male beauty. He was wearing his customary jeans—the tight, cowboy kind that were worn in all the right places—and a shirt whose rolled-up sleeves emphasized the strength of his forearms. His hair was disheveled, and his eyes were solemn as they stared back at her.

She wanted to ask where he'd been and knew she didn't have the right.

"How's he doing?" Dylan asked, though he came no closer.

She couldn't have stopped her smile if her life had depended on it. "He's fine. Starving. Would you like to hold him?"

Panic filled his eyes. "Uh, no thanks. I'm not very good at it. How does pizza sound for dinner?"

"Good." *Way to go, Chantal. Keep up the brilliant conversation and you'll run him off for sure.* She propped Brady up and started patting him on the back. "I was getting worried about you." It was as close as she could get to asking where he'd gone.

"I took a cab over to Darlene Gardener's to pick up my car. I'll have to take it back tomorrow."

Chantal wasn't prepared for the sharp shaft of pain that stabbed her heart. "You're leaving tomorrow?"

He couldn't quite meet her eyes and attempted a smile. "Yeah. I don't want to wear out my welcome." He waved a hand toward her and the baby. "How long until you're finished?"

"Not long."

"I'll order the pizza, then."

"Good." Her heart felt like a leaden weight in her chest. Dylan was going back to New Jersey. Somehow, she'd expected him to stay and spend some time with her and the baby.

Ask him to stay. The inner voice urged her to do her heart's bidding, but she knew she couldn't. If he refused, she would be humiliated. Devastated. There was no way she could put herself in that position again. She watched him leave the room with a sinking heart. She was right in the middle of a no-win situation.

Dinner was a quiet ordeal. Dylan was withdrawn, unapproachable. Chantal was torn between irritation at herself and him and an undeniable sadness. She wondered if he was hurting, and told herself not to be foolish. Dylan hadn't asked for any of this. When he finished cleaning the kitchen, she fixed Brady's bottles and decided she might as well call it a night. The openness they'd shared the past two nights was nowhere in sight.

"I'm going to bed," she said. "I'm exhausted." *Are you coming?*

Dylan hardly glanced up from the newspaper. "There's a good Western coming on at nine. I think I'll watch it."

"Oh."

After making sure that Brady was all right, Chantal went to bed but not to sleep. Though Dylan turned the television's volume low, she could hear the roar of the gunfights, the occasional whinnying of a horse and the low thrum of voices. She fell asleep, wondering how she'd ever be able to sleep without Dylan next to her.

* * *

Chantal awoke with a start. Rubbing her eyes, she looked at the glowing green numerals of the bedside clock. Almost feeding time. Glancing at the other side of the bed, she saw that Dylan wasn't there. She could still hear the television, and the soft glow of a table lamp cast a faint light through the bedroom doorway. He must have fallen asleep watching his movie. Rising slowly, sleepily she made her way to the antique cradle where Brady slept.

It was empty! She felt as if her knees would crumple beneath her weight. Panic stole her breath. She took a step toward the living room; her mouth opened to call for Dylan. Dylan. Suddenly she stopped. Reason returned. Dylan was here. She and the baby were safe.

Drawn by curiosity, her legs growing steadier by the moment, she crossed the small room to the sofa and peered over the back. The sight she beheld brought a lump of emotion to her throat. Half seating herself on the sofa back, she gazed her fill.

Dylan slept on his back, Brady was asleep on his chest. Dylan's big hand was splayed across the baby's back in a protective gesture, and his lips brushed the top of his son's head. Brady's right hand—incredibly small and white—rested against Dylan's whisker-rough cheek in what looked like a gentle caress. She wondered if her father had ever held her while she slept. She wondered if Dylan's had.

Tears filled her eyes and resolution filled her heart. She couldn't let Dylan leave, not without at least trying to convince him to stay. She owed Brady that much. Boys needed fathers. All children needed fathers—good fathers. There was no doubt in her mind that Dylan would be the best.

There was no doubt about something else, too, something Chantal has been afraid to acknowledge. *She* needed Dylan. What had started out in Atlantic City as a simple celebration of life and a brief, exciting sexual excursion had developed into love. Asking herself how it had happened would be useless. She only knew that it had.

A lot of people would say it was too soon, that she hardly knew him, but as he'd once said, as Gracie had once said: she knew enough. She knew that Dylan Garvey could be trusted. With her life. With her heart.

He'd come when she'd called him to help find the baby. He'd been there for her when she came home from the hospital. He'd given her her son, her happiness, back. The same son she knew he needed to secure his own happiness.

Okay, so he wasn't affectionate, but she understood that, now, too, just as she understood his reluctance to hold the baby. She knew that if he kept people at arm's length, he felt the less likely he was to be hurt. Like her, Dylan had suffered his share of rejections. Like her, he had to learn to trust. Maybe it was a lesson they could learn together. The problem was convincing him that it was a worthwhile goal.

Brady wriggled and gave a sleepy wail. Chantal smiled. He was right on schedule. Dylan shifted. Quietly, being careful not to wake either of them, she tiptoed back to the bedroom. She eased back down on the bed with a contented feeling warming her. Dylan could handle the feeding and the diaper changing. And she was sure he wanted to.

*   *   *

Dylan was in the bathroom taking his shaving gear from the medicine chest when Chantal cornered him. She'd taken special pains with her hair and makeup and was wearing a shorts outfit that Shiloh claimed did wonders for her coloring. Forcing a smile to her lips, she wiped her sweating palms down the baggy legs of the shorts and tried to remember the speech she'd been rehearsing all morning. She had to do this right. She was sacrificing her fear of rejection on the altar of her love for Dylan. Her future and Brady's depended on how well she handled the next few minutes.

Dylan was looking at her with a curious expression, a can of shaving cream in his hand.

She opened her mouth to say all the practiced words, all the carefully executed phrases that would play on his sympathies and tug at his heartstrings. Instead, a single word came out.

"Stay."

His dark eyes mirrored his shock and a faint, reluctant hope. "What?"

Chantal took a step closer and placed her hand on his bare forearm. "Stay in Louisiana and make a family with me and Brady," she said, a quaver in her voice, her heart in her eyes. "He needs a father. I need a husband."

Dylan swallowed. He set the shaving cream in the sink and held up his hands. "I've spilled blood with these hands, Chantal. And I'll likely spill more before I die."

Chantal reached and took both his hands in hers. "They're gentle hands, Dylan. Strong hands. The kind of hands I'm not afraid to let shape my life and Brady's."

Dylan shook his head and blew out a long breath.

"We've both had some bad experiences," she continued. "Maybe marriage is like child rearing. Maybe we won't make those mistakes again. Maybe we'll make new ones. But the important thing is that maybe, with Brady's help, we can learn how to give more of ourselves and become a better family than what either of us had. Maybe, we can slay the dragons and learn to trust . . . together."

"Why?" Dylan asked. "Why me, out of all the men you've known? Why trust me?"

A soft smile curved Chantal's lips. "I really didn't have much choice," she said. "Love and trust go hand in hand."

"Love?"

She nodded. "I love you. It happened sort of like Brady. I didn't plan it. I didn't want it. But I have it right here." She brought both of his hands to her heart. "And I have a feeling it will bring me as much happiness as Brady already has."

Something dark and dangerous entered his eyes. He started to say something.

"Don't say anything, yet. Just think about it. Maybe, if you decide to stay, someday you'll learn to love me, too."

In a gesture that stole her breath, Dylan lifted his hands and cradled her face between his gentle palms. His sexy mouth curved into one of those watch-out-heart smiles.

"Impossible," he told her, lowering his mouth to hers. "I already do."

Epilogue

The July sun that had long before burned away the morning mists was now busy seeking out the rare openings in the leafy canopy of oak leaves. It mottled the patchwork quilt spread beneath and dappled the faces of Dylan and Brady, both fast asleep on its wash-faded surface. A breath of hot air stirred the leaves and riffled Dylan's hair.

As it always did when she looked at her husband, Chantal's heart swelled with so much love and pride that it was almost painful. In spite of his reservations, Dylan Garvey was the best thing that had ever happened to her. The thought that they might have missed each other was frightening. So was the knowledge that if she hadn't buried her fears and proposed to him, their old hurts and misplaced pride might have kept them from the two years of happiness they'd shared.

Today was Brady's second birthday. Later in the day the event would be celebrated with a picnic. Everyone was coming: Gracie, Cade and Shiloh—who was pregnant again—and Shiloh's brother, Garrett, his wife, Molly, and their two children. The picnic would be followed by a fireworks display. When Chantal pointed out that Dylan had purchased more fireworks than the town of Thibodaux had exploded on July fourth he had justified his extravagance by reminding her how much Brady loved the fireworks display. And afterall, it wasn't every day a boy turned two.

Chantal was still smiling at the memory when Brady stirred and whimpered, opening his sleep-glazed eyes. Smiling and murmuring to him in a soft voice so she wouldn't wake Dylan, Chantal leaned over and scooped him into her arms. He burrowed as close as her seven-months-pregnant tummy would allow. The thought that she and Dylan were going to have another baby was a warm feeling deep inside her. She had no regrets abut marrying him, and doubted she ever would.

After Dylan had brought Brady home and agreed to marry her, she had gotten him to the altar as soon as possible, telling him he needed to make an honest woman out of her. He had quit his job in Atlantic City and been snapped up by the Thibodaux police, much to Phil Rousseau's pleasure. The detective and Dylan had become fast friends. Dylan had also grown close to Cade and to Garrett Rambler, which pleased Chantal greatly.

It was a good life they now shared in Gracie's old two-story farmhouse, but Chantal was too much of a realist to pretend their life together was perfect. Since neither of them were perfect people that was an unrealistic expectation. They were both growing, though, sloughing off the fears and habits of the past and concentrating on making each other happy and fulfilled. There were times Dylan was short and ill-tempered, and there were also times Chantal knew she closed herself up from him. The difference was that with Darlene Gardener's help they were learning that those times would pass and that the other person was there for them . . . only an arm's length away.

"A 'quirrel," Brady said, interrupting Chantal's thoughts. He pointed a chubby finger at a gray squirrel clinging to the trunk of a tree several yards away, his tail twitching nervously.

"A big squirrel," Chantal said.

"I wanna see." Pulling free, he slid from her lap and wandered across the wide expanse of grass.

"He's getting pretty independent, isn't he?"

Chantal glanced over at Dylan who was propped on one elbow, regarding their son with what could only be described as pure masculine pride.

"He surely is," she agreed. "I'm sorry we woke you."

"You didn't." He smothered a yawn and levered himself to a sitting position, crossing his denim-covered legs Indian style. "I guess I got my nap out."

He patted the place next to him and Chantal scooted closer, laying her head on his shoulder. "Did you sleep?"

"No. I watched you and Brady sleep and thought about how lucky I am to have you both."

"No regrets?"

"Just one." She felt him stiffen and lifted her head to meet his troubled gaze. "I wish we could have met sooner. I wish we'd had more time together."

The tension in Dylan vanished as quickly as it had come. "Maybe we weren't ready for each other until we did meet. Besides, we've got plenty of time to spend together. Years."

"I know."

"Mama! Daddy! The 'quirrel runned away!" Brady called, turning and starting toward them as fast as his legs could cover the uneven ground.

"He sure did!" A smile wreathed Dylan's rugged features.

Brady was less than half a dozen yards away when his toe caught on something and he went sprawling, renting the quiet afternoon with an ear-splitting wail.

Dylan started to get to his feet; Chantal put a restraining hand on his arm.

"Hop up, Brady! Come and let Mama see," she called. Still crying, Brady stood and started toward them.

Dylan gave her a questioning look. "He's fine, honey," she assured him. "He's more mad about falling than he is hurt."

"How do you know?"

"I know," she said with the inate wisdom of mothers everywhere. "If I went running every time he fell down I'd spend most of my time doing nothing else. I'd race you to him, if I thought he was really hurt."

Brady sauntered onto the quilt, knuckling the tears from his dark eyes.

"Are you okay, buddy?" Dylan asked.

Brady looked down at his bare, grass-stained knees. A thin line of blood indicated a superficial scratch. He gave a mighty sniff. "I gotta boo-boo."

Dylan held out his arms. "Come here and let Daddy kiss it all better."

"Daddys don't kiss it better. Mamas do."

"Sure daddys kiss it better," Dylan said, pulling the boy onto his lap and examining his scrapes.

A memory from the past flitted through Chantal's mind. The memory of Dylan telling her how when he'd been hurt as a child he'd crawled up into his father's lap only to be told to to get down . . . go away. That was a disappointment Brady would never have to face.

"Isn't that right, Mom?"

Dylan's question dragged Chantal back from the past. "Isn't what right?"

He looped an arm around her shoulders and took her lips in a kiss that stole her breath and sent her nerve endings asizzle.

"Don't daddys know how to kiss it and make it all better?"

A bemused expression softened Chantal's features. She thought of how his kisses set her senses aflame and how his steadfastness made her feel safe and unafraid to face tomorrow. "I don't know about all daddys, Brady," she said, bestowing her smile on them both, "but your daddy certainly does."

She watched as Brady let Dylan kiss both knees, watched as he tickled their son until he rolled on the quilt in a gale of giggles.

She felt a sudden sorrow for Patrick Garvey, and for Dylan's former wife. They'd never known him at all. Never known what depths of sensitivity lay hidden behind his facade of hardness.

Dylan Garvey wasn't cold and hardhearted at all. He was just a man who needed lots of loving. Her man. Her love.

* * * * *

EXTRA, EXTRA!
Watch for Bay Matthews's next book from
Silhouette Special Edition, due out in the fall
of 1994. You'll have to keep a lookout, because
Bay has decided to write under her real name,
Penny Richards. Don't miss this exciting new
book by Penny Richards!

A Note From The Author

I liked writing about Chantal because she's a real person—one with faults (stubborn, a bit too independent, a tendency to shut herself off) as well as virtues (family-oriented, hard worker, warm-hearted). Even though she's come through some hard times, she's learned to pick up the pieces and get on with her life, something she's done more than once. And even though she was abandoned by her father and hurt by her ex-husband, she never lost sight of one of the most important things, one of the greatest sources of a person's strength: the love of her family.

The disappointments Chantal had experienced forced her to take on a lot of responsibility at an early age, but it also taught her the value of giving a good day's work. The trials she's been through have made her cautious, but that only helps her in separating the gold from the dross, which is how she can see beyond the tough-guy act that Dylan and Gracie both put on. In short, her upbringing has made her strong and hardworking, loving, thrifty and creative, attributes that were as much a part of our grandmothers' lives as they are a part of the lives of the women of today.

Chantal is independent—strong enough to make it on her own but realizing that her life will be more complete with the right man at her side, a lesson I think all of us who love a good love story have learned.

Sincerely,

Bay Matthews
(aka Penny Richards)

SALLY JANE GOT MARRIED
Celeste Hamilton

Everyone believed Sally Jane Haskins was the town bad girl—except widowed father Cotter Graham. When a night of passion suddenly meant they were expecting, a trip down the aisle was the only choice. Sally Jane hoped that this, at last, was her chance at happily ever after....

Celebrate Sally Jane's nuptials in Celeste Hamilton's SALLY JANE GOT MARRIED, available in February.

She's friend, wife, mother—she's you! And beside each Special Woman stands a wonderfully *special* man. It's a celebration of our heroines—and the men who become part of their lives.

Don't miss **THAT SPECIAL WOMAN!** each month— from some of your special authors! Only from Silhouette Special Edition!

TSW294

He staked his claim...

HONOR BOUND

by
New York Times
Bestselling Author

previously published under the pseudonym Erin St. Claire

As Aislinn Andrews opened her mouth to scream, a hard
hand clamped over her face and she found herself face-
to-face with Lucas Greywolf, a lean, lethal-looking
Navajo and escaped convict who swore he wouldn't hurt
her— *if* she helped him.

Look for HONOR BOUND at your favorite
retail outlet this January.

Only from...

And now for something completely different from Silhouette....

SPELLBOUND
ROMANCE

Unique and innovative stories that take you into the world of paranormal happenings. Look for our special "Spellbound" flash—and get ready for a truly exciting reading experience!

In February, look for
One Unbelievable Man **(SR #993)**
by Pat Montana.

Was he man or myth? Cass Kohlmann's mysterious traveling companion, Michael O'Shea, had her all confused. He'd suddenly appeared, claiming she was his destiny—determined to win her heart. But could levelheaded Cass learn to believe in fairy tales...before her fantasy man disappeared forever?

Don't miss the charming, sexy and utterly mysterious Michael O'Shea in
ONE UNBELIEVABLE MAN.
Watch for him in February—only from

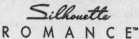

Silhouette
R O M A N C E ™

SPELL2

CONVINCING ALEX

Those Wild Ukrainians

Look who Detective Alex Stanislaski has picked up....

When soap opera writer Bess McNee hit the streets in spandex pants and a clinging tube-top in order to research the role of a prostitute, she was looking for trouble—but not too much trouble.

Then she got busted by straight-laced Detective Alex Stanislaski and found a lot more than she'd bargained for. This man wasn't buying anything she said, and Bess realized she was going to have to be a *lot* more convincing....

If you enjoyed TAMING NATASHA (SE #583), LURING A LADY (SE #709) and FALLING FOR RACHEL (SE #810), then be sure to read CONVINCING ALEX, the delightful tale of another one of THOSE WILD UKRAINIANS finding love where it's least expected.

SSENR

FIVE UNIQUE SERIES
FOR EVERY WOMAN YOU ARE...

Silhouette ROMANCE™

Tender, passionate, heartwarming stories that will move you with the wonder of love, time and again. It's romance, the way you always knew it could be.

SILHOUETTE *Desire* ®

Red-hot is what we've got! Sparkling, scintillating, *sensuous* love stories. Once you pick up one you won't be able to put it down...only in Silhouette Desire.

Silhouette SPECIAL EDITION ®

Stories of love and life, these powerful novels are tales that you can identify with—romances with "something special" added in! Silhouette Special Edition is entertainment for the heart.

SILHOUETTE·INTIMATE·MOMENTS ®

Enter a world where passions run hot and excitement is always high. Dramatic, larger than life and always compelling—Silhouette Intimate Moments provides captivating romance to cherish forever.

SILHOUETTE *Shadows*

She's strong, she's smart—she's you. Join her for a walk on the dark side of love, where undying passion is always waiting...in the shadows.

Silhouette, where passion lives.